KILLIAN'S CANYON

**Center Point
Large Print**

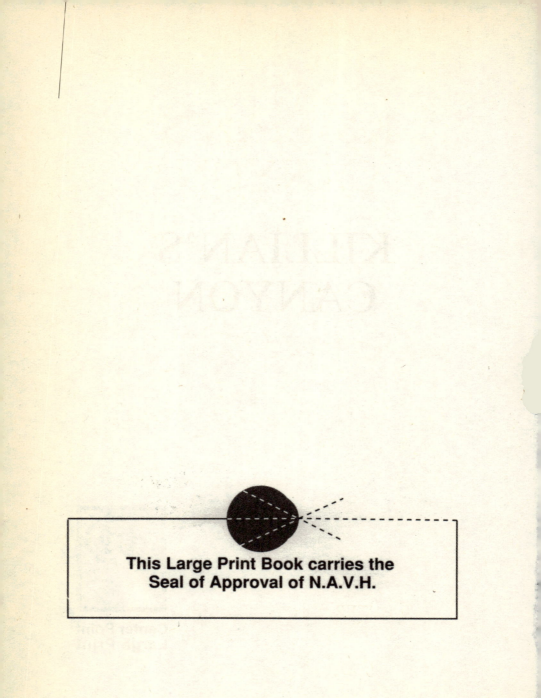

**This Large Print Book carries the
Seal of Approval of N.A.V.H.**

KILLIAN'S CANYON

LAURAN PAINE

CENTER POINT PUBLISHING
THORNDIKE, MAINE

This Center Point Large Print edition
is published in the year 2006 by arrangement with
Golden West Literary Agency.

The text of this Large Print edition is unabridged. In other
aspects, this book may vary from the original edition. Printed in
Thailand. Set in 16-point Times New Roman type.

ISBN 1-58547-792-3

Library of Congress Cataloging-in-Publication Data

Paine, Lauran.
   Killian's canyon / Lauran Paine.--Center Point large print ed.
      p. cm.
   ISBN 1-58547-792-3 (lib. bdg. : alk. paper)
   1. Large type books. I. Title.

PS3566.A34K554 2006
813'.54--dc22
                                                      2006001854

KILLIAN'S CANYON

1

A World Apart

Winter had passed but the winds of spring came directly over the snow-layered Rocky Mountains. It was as the old drifter said, who lived in the log cabin Killian had built when he first came to Colorado's high country, colder than a witch's teat.

A man could pile on plenty of clothing, but as the drifter had often remarked, even with a woollen blanket-coat, two shirts, a muffler and long-johns beneath a man's britches, the cold wind came through to chill the marrow in a man's bones.

Killian was younger, he had patiently out-waited five winters and springs and while the cold was as bitter as original sin, he minded it less than he minded the wind.

He told the drifter one evening inside his larger cabin, the one he'd completed the year before the old man arrived, half-starved and skinny as a snake, during the hottest time of summer a man could cool off in the little pool made by the spring, and in winter he could keep warm inside the cabins with a fire in the rock-work at the east end of both cabins where there was a fireplace, but there was not a blessed thing a man could do about wind but wait it out, and that wasn't always easy, not in Colorado's high country. It arrived without warning, sometimes blew for days, came from different directions, which wore a man out changing directions as he braced into it.

The old man, who had told Killian his name was Ambrose Wright, was blessed with a fine set of teeth, otherwise his age was indeterminate. His face was as weathered and lined as an old piece of leather, and his sinewy build made him almost inexhaustible even if he had been a young man, and while Killian had never asked his age he guessed it to be in the seventies.

The old man never talked about himself. He was, however, talkative on any other subject and in fact the longer they shared the canyon the more Killian was impressed by the old man's knowledge. Sometime in his life he had done it all, at least once, from knowing the precise angle for notching logs, to tracking the cougar who tried to kill Killian's saddle animal.

George Killian was in his prime, of middle height with hair that was light. The old man said it was strawberry roan. Killian might weather in time but in his prime he was fair-skinned, blue-eyed, tough as old rawhide, and had come from Ireland. He did not say when, but if an Irish accent might have supported that, he had no accent at all.

Why he had come to the high country was no particular mystery. Free land for the taking, federal law which allowed a man to file for a homestead on 160 acres. There was a good spring in his canyon, plenty of livestock feed, and the right to graze animals over hundreds of acres of unclaimed federal land.

Killian's canyon had three high hills, north, east and west. Southward the land was open with a view of grass and timber country as far, and farther, than a man could see. Those fierce springtime winds were somewhat blunted from the north. Not entirely but somewhat.

In old Ambrose's frequent wanderings, with an old Sharps carbine which enabled him to return more often than not with camp meat, he had got to know the round-about country very well, including all of Killian's canyon and beyond.

One fiercely windy, cold evening while the old man and Killian were having supper at George's log house, Ambrose indifferently mentioned climbing a northerly hill and seeing several camp-fires in the distance. Killian, who had also scouted the countryside, but on horseback, was interested. He had never seen indications of other humans and he had been living in his highland hideout for five years.

Old Ambrose lowered his tin coffee cup looking directly at George when he said, 'In'ians,' and proceeded to empty the cup before also saying, 'A man don't have to scout 'em up. In'ians make ragged camps, they keep dogs'n horses and they make a lot of noise.'

Killian leaned back off the pine-bough table with his back to the fire. 'The army rounded 'em up years ago. Herded 'em on to reservations. I've been here better'n five years, rode the hills from here to there an' never saw an Indian.'

Ambrose's faded, pale eyes considered the younger man with bitter humor. 'Ride the horse north an' a little west tomorrow. If the wind's blowin' right you'll smell their smoke. If you see 'em, I'd keep to cover . . . I know, they been whipped by the army, they're wore down and poorly, but don't make no mistake about In'ians, they've killed lot of folks an' buried 'em that nobody ever found.'

The old man ate a while, refilled his cup from the speckleware pot on the wood stove, sat back down and said, 'Too bad you ain't a drinkin' man, George. On a night like this nothin' eases the nerves like Irish coffee.'

Killian had no whiskey, and although he had come from a family of accomplished brewers he was not much of a drinking man. When every penny he had was used to buy necessities, while he had nothing against whiskey, he very rarely brought a bottle back from the trading post nine miles south-east, a place called Bridgerville.

Ambrose sat holding his tin cup gazing past the younger man at the fire when he quietly said, 'Crows or 'Rapahoes. This was their country.' He smiled into the fire. 'Puttin' In'ians on a reservation is fine, 'ceptin' there's always holdouts. A man can't blame 'em. They lived free for hunnerts of years, an' all of a sudden they get fought to a standstill, rounded up an' herded to some place where whites don't want the land.'

Ambrose drifted off into silence.

Killian also refilled his cup, sat at the table full as a tick of antelope meat regarding the old man. He dryly said, 'That kind of talk can get you lynched in the settlements.'

Ambrose brought his faded eyes back to the younger man. 'George, I didn't get close but I've seen it before. Stragglin' bands of 'em ridin' bony horses, wearin' ragged clothes, armed with old guns that don't shoot half the time, stealin' on the outskirts of towns, hidin' like outlaws.' At the steady gaze Killian was putting on the old man, Ambrose also said, 'I ain't no In'ian lover by a damned sight, but what's happenin' to 'em is *dina sica* the same as it would happen to us if the boot was on the other foot.'

They sat until there was a lull in the wind then Ambrose returned to his own cabin, one room with a stone fireplace and several cupboards as well as an iron army cot.

Killian had been fully occupied building his second, larger cabin with four rooms, a snug kitchen, and furniture he had crafted by hand. His intention was to acquire livestock, but that was more likely to remain a dream than a goal. He had no money with which to buy animals. What money that had come his way since he'd homestead in his canyon was from labour he did for others, more often than not at Bridgerville where he made furniture which was not otherwise available. He also slatted roofs, did whatever came his way. In Bridgerville the mercantile proprietor, a nearly bald man with an ample belly and the massive gold watch-chain to span it, was helpful. He liked George. He also had a very pale, plump daughter who wore her straw-colored hair in pigtails, the storekeeper wanted to marry off, but only to some young man who was of good habits, did not drink, and gave a good day's work for his money.

George liked the girl, they were friends, but she wanted a husband, not someone who visited the settlement maybe two or three times a year.

Killian and old Ambrose had made it through another winter but were low on necessities Mother Nature did not provide. When he told Ambrose he would go to the settlement directly, the old man nodded without saying that in his opinion if folks needed sugar all they had to do was find a bee tree, if they wanted flour they could improvise from hammered bean plants, tobacco was available from *kinnikinik*.

If a man had to and was of a mind, he could live well without going near settlements. Ambrose had spent years avoiding them; he had learned Indian ways, but except when necessary he did nothing to alter Killian's ways.

Even when George went out a-horseback to find those tomahawks Ambrose had seen, beyond warning the younger man about avoiding contact and never letting the horse out of his sight, the old man watched Killian leave the canyon, and spent the day jerking meat for winter. Ambrose Wright's life was divided into two periods, the warm times when men hunted and stored up, and winters when they ate what they had put by.

One time long ago Ambrose had visited the camp of wagoners bound for Oregon. A preacher sat by the fire after all but Ambrose had departed, and said human existence had always been and still was belly-orientated.

Ambrose never forgot that. He might have reached the same conclusion if he'd ever thought about it. For a fact Ambrose had spent most of his life hunting, first buffalo and when they became scarce, deer, antelope, wild turkeys, wild pigs, and an assortment of other edible creatures.

He was still working with the jerked meat, skiving it into long strips to be peppered and placed atop the cabin's roof to cure in sunlight, when Killian returned, soberly cared for the horse and came over to Ambrose's cabin, where he got a dipperful of water, sat on a bench against the wall and while watching the old man work, said, 'You were right. It's a fair-sized band. Stragglin' over the countryside keepin' mostly to timber.'

'Any idea how many?' the old man asked.

'I'd guess maybe thirty, all told.'

Ambrose made a clucking sound as he made thin slices. 'It used to be a hunnert an' more when they moved.'

Ambrose straightened back to consider his strips of meat, reached for a pepper pot and began liberally sprinkling. As he did this he smiled. 'Feller told me one time to use lots of pepper. That way a man couldn't tell which was pepper specks an' where the flies been.'

Killian said, 'They aren't moving.'

Ambrose kept sprinkling. 'They will. They got to. Nobody wants In'ians around. It ain't exactly that they're afraid of 'em, they just plain don't like 'em.

Folks see their smoke or a camp an' they'll bust their buttons to find the army and guide it back.'

But the Indians did not leave. Ten days later Ambrose took his old army carbine and told George he was going hunting. If George had been as old as Ambrose he would have known better. One gunshot within hearing distance of hide-out redskins would be like kicking a hornets' nest.

When Ambrose returned at dusk, he leaned his weapon aside, sat down and said, 'Your next trip to Bridgerville fetch back a bottle of whiskey.'

Killian turned from the wood stove where he was frying meat, looked long at the old man and said, 'I'll do it. You look tuckered.'

Ambrose gazed stonily at the younger man as he spoke. 'There's whites among them In'ians.'

'White men?'

Ambrose nodded. 'When you see somethin' like that you lock your doors at night. In'ians don't draw no line. They take in white men. George, looked to me like maybe six or eight of 'em. Mostly it's been my experience the only whiteskins that join In'ians is rene-gades, an' partner, that many of 'em among them In'ians out yonder means night raids an' worse.' Ambrose wrinkled his nose as Killian put meat on two tin plates atop the table. The old man got himself a cup of spring water from the bucket, took it to the table with him and sat down to pick up a knife in one hand, a fork in the other hand as he waited until Killian was seated to say the rest of it. 'There was tracks. They

14

been there long enough. In'ians always scout up a country.'

Killian gazed steadily at the old man. 'They've seen our cabins?'

'Sure as I'm settin' here. If it was just stragglin' hide-outs I'd say give 'em time an' they'd move on, but them tracks sort of made the hair on the back of my neck stand up. They scouted up your canyon. Most likely they scouted for miles around. To me that means them renegade whites got somethin' in mind besides hidin' out . . . I've seen what men like that do to isolated homesteads an' ranches, sometimes to villages if there's enough of 'em.'

George ate in silence for a while then said, 'You have any idea where the nearest soldiers would be?'

Ambrose hadn't any idea. 'You been here longer'n me,' he said, and went to work on his meat. After a while he also said, 'The folks at Bridgerville might want to know there's a mixed band of renegade whites and hide-out In'ians in the country. . . . When fellers like that start out raidin', they do it like wildfire. Raid every isolated place they can in a day or two, kill every-thin' that moves, set fires an' leave like they're ridin' the wind. By the time soldiers or townsmen get after them, they're plumb gone.' Ambrose finished eating, wiped his mouth with a soiled sleeve and bleakly smiled. 'We'll be first. They scouted us up real proper. Boot tracks an' moccasin tracks.' His bleak smile widened. 'What they'll leave is two burnt cabins with you'n me in them.'

15

Killian leaned back, his meal was only half eaten. All he knew about Indians could have been put on a pin head without any crowding. He had of course heard all the grisly stories and while he'd seen many Indians, with no reason to go among them; he did not know a Crow or an Arapaho from a south desert Apache or an eastern seaboard Pequot.

He finally said, 'I'll ride to the settlement.'

Ambrose gazed dispassionately at the younger man as he said, 'Good idea.' He did not mention what bothered him, which was simply that as many scouting-up tracks as he'd seen, he was convinced an attack on Killian's canyon could come any time, and while Indians as a rule avoided fighting after dark, white renegades had no such inhibitions.

He did say, very dryly, as he arose to take plates to the wash bucket, that if George could get out the south end of the canyon he could probably make it down to Bridgerville.

They cleaned up in silence before Killian took his rifle down from its wall pegs, hitched the belt-gun around his middle and put on a coat. Old Ambrose sat down, produced a nearly burned-out little pipe, filled it with half *kinnikinik,* half tobacco and fired it up.

Killian said, 'You got to hide.'

The old man nodded and puffed. There was no place to hide where fire could not find him. He removed the pipe, crossed to the door, stood listening for a long time then turned and said, 'If tonight's the night, partner, you'll never get to the south end of the canyon,' and shoved out a rough and calloused hand.

They shook. When Killian would have walked out of the cabin Ambrose pushed him back, crossed to the candles, snuffed each one out, returned to the doorway, said, 'Wait,' and slipped outside.

There was a moon, a sickly, lop-sided thing that shed almost no light downward.

Ambrose soundlessly scouted the area around the cabins, even went out a little beyond and scouted.

He was beginning to take heart as he turned back when two owls hooted, one along the east side of the canyon, the other one on the west side.

Ambrose stopped stone still. There were owls in the canyon, had been ever since he'd been there and those calls had sounded exactly like owls, but any talented imitator could made owl sounds.

He made his way slowly, soundlessly and carefully back to the cabin, pushed Killian clear of the door and closed it at his back. He didn't mention the owl sounds. He said, 'Lead the horse, keep in shadows. Good thing the horse ain't shod . . . George, I always heard Irishmen was good prayin' folks. Well, if that's so now'd be a good time . . . I didn't see nothin' but when you get my age an' have lived through, you develop what folks call sixth sense. I got that feelin' now. They're out there.'

Killian nodded in the gloom. 'Next time we run for it. Ambrose, we'll both ride if I got to steal a horse. I don't like the idea of leaving you here alone.'

The old man's strong teeth showed in the darkness.

'Did I ever tell you I knew how to be invisible? Now, go on, listen, keep to shadows—an' pray. It never done me much good but it might work for you. . . . Lead the horse, don't get on him for half the distance. They can sky-line a mounted man. Walk slow, don't make no noise . . . George. . . .'

'Ambrose I don't like leaving.'

The old man snarled, 'Go! Warn them settlement folks. *Now, dammit go!*'

2

For Lack of a Window

Ambrose was dead right about one thing, the renegades and their bronco Indians had indeed scouted for miles. They had pinpointed every isolated homestead and ranch to within a couple of miles of Bridgerville which they had also assessed, but the village was too large so they had turned back all the way to their hidden camp in the timber. The first place to be raided was in a canyon which was funnel-shaped, rough highlands on three sides and wide open southward. There were two cabins which they had watched belly-down for several days, until satisfied only two people lived there. One young, roan-haired man and one wizened, wiry old man.

Killian's, being due southward, would be the first place they would attack. There were two scouts, one easterly, one westerly. They were to watch the cabins until after moon-rise, when the other raiders would appear. Those two scouts kept in touch by imitating the sounds of owls.

The night was poorly lighted, thick shadows were settled in the canyon. For a while there was candlelight in the larger cabin. Later there was light in the smaller log house and none in the larger cabin.

It was customary among renegades to make one of their whirlwind attacks after the last light had been extinguished.

In this instance it was not extinguished even after the entire raiding band was on the heights above the canyon. One of the renegade whites, a large, thick man with dark eyes and a beard, whose name was Pickett, Hendry Pickett, stood looking down and worrying a cud of tobacco in one cheek.

Hendry Pickett was notorious in the southwest. When it got too hot for him down yonder he and several other renegades went north, found safety among a traveling band of Crows, and for more than two years had raided, killed and plundered. Mostly, their attacks were eventually discovered, usually by smoke rising into a clear sky the morning after.

Eventually even the army was roiled, but mostly it was isolated ranchers and villagers who worried. But as long as the raids occurred in southern Colorado, people near the Wyoming line in upper Colorado, while they heard of the ferocity of the attacks, did not worry. Hundreds of miles separated those two areas of the state.

The army, however, took all raids seriously. Even up north they had scouts and patrols circulating, but the soldiers were headquartered in the south where previous raids had occurred. Northerly patrolling was considered perfunctory. Not every officer was convinced the raids in the south, which abruptly stopped, did not mean the roving renegades had moved northward and after a long winter had passed without more raids, even the seasoned renegade-hunters were not convinced the raiders had not disappeared down over the line into Mexico. What supported that position was that raids by marauding bands south of the border seemed to increase. Still, as hard-bitten old campaigners occasionally pointed out, there were always raids and uprisings in Mexico which did not have to mean the marauders from up north in southern Colorado had gone south.

None of this was exactly news to Ambrose Wright, who knew something of raiding, nor as clouds occasionally scudded across that puny moon, did he think of anything beyond Killian's canyon and survival.

He allowed the candle to burn down on the theory that if raiders were out there, they would hold off attacking a place where folks might be awake—with weapons handy.

The night advanced. Ambrose wished he had left candles burning in Killian's cabin too, but he hadn't and his chance of getting over there to rekindle candles were about the same as the survival of a snowball in hell.

The longer he waited, rifle across his knees, holstered hawgleg on his right hip, the stronger became his sixth sense. He had no illusions, one man with a rifle and pistol might prolong things but against a seasoned band of raiders his chances of surviving would require a miracle, and to his knowledge such things did not happen.

Whiskey would have helped. He thought back down the years. He'd had his share of narrow squeaks. After several of them he had scars to remind him of when and where those fights had happened.

He stoked the foul little pipe, fired it up from the candle and sat still in shadows straining to pick up every sound. If he 'went' he did not figure to go alone.

Once, he had hidden for three days in a root cellar from ransacking Secesh soldiers. Afterwards even the sight of a rutabaga made his innards recoil.

Killian and he had discussed digging a root cellar. That had been about a year ago. Ambrose smiled in the shadows. They had argued about the location and the size. In the end they had let the topic die. It wouldn't have made much difference anyway. Greenhorn raiders might overlook a cellar, seasoned raiders never would.

He got a drink of water, refilled the pipe and puffed up a tangy-scented small cloud. By his estimate it was close to midnight. What pleased him at a time when few things could have, was that he had heard no southward gunfire. George had got clear of the funnel end of the canyon.

He smoked, watched the dying candle and waited. For a feller who learned quick, wasn't afraid of asking questions and was young enough to some day make his mark west of the Missouri despite being a foreigner,

George was learning the ways of survival in a land, unlike the place he had come from, with no law other than the kind every man carried in his hand or on his hip. Where men drank whiskey—which George didn't seem to care for—and never took an In'ian to wife.

Old Ambrose had wandered, had known men who, like Gabe Bridger, were larger than life, and who were also dead.

His reverie was broken by the sound of someone wearing boots approaching from the north. Ambrose knocked out the pipe but otherwise did not move. Whoever was out there and who was making noise as he walked, was doing it deliberately.

It wasn't an Indian, they didn't wear boots nor were they bold enough to allow themselves to be heard on a dark, quiet night.

Ambrose knew about what was going to happen, he had experienced the same thing, with variations, in his lifetime.

When the walking man was close enough, he arose, went to the only window and leaning from one side, looked out for movement.

What he saw was a lean man in filthy buckskins who had a drooping feather hanging from one side of his hat. The man was carrying a Winchester carbine in the crook of one arm. When he stopped mid-way between the cabins, he looked left and right, southward, then called out.

'Anybody here? My name's Walter Kinkaid, I'm a trader 'n trapper. . . . Anyone here?'

Ambrose eased his gun out slowly and silently. The man dressed as a white Indian made an excellent target. He faced toward Ambrose's cabin, the only place where light was showing, and called again. 'I need a place to bed down. I been livin' up north. There's a settlement south-easterly where I figure to get supplies. . . . Anyone hear me?'

Ambrose answered without raising his voice, with the gun-butt snugged back, with his finger curled inside the trigger-guard and with the stranger centered in his sights.

'Yes sir, there's someone here. More'n one but the others is bedded down. Walk toward the light, Mister Kinkaid. I can't make you out very well.'

The man in buckskin faced the area of Ambrose's light.

'Didn't mean to wake you up, friend. . . . Is the others awake?'

'I think they're stirrin'. Walk toward me—friend.'

Kinkaid still did not move. 'How many is in there with you?'

Ambrose made a mistake, but he lied with a clear conscience. 'Four. Walk toward me, Mister Kinkaid.'

The stranger with the drooping feather broadly smiled. 'I'll get my pack animal and come back,' he said, and would have walked away if Ambrose hadn't stopped him. 'Leave the pack animal be . . . walk toward me!'

The lean man seemed to have taken root, but he made a little fluttery gesture with one hand. 'I can't leave the critter tied up out yonder. He's wore down.'

Ambrose cocked the gun. *'Walk toward me you son of a bitch!'*

Kinkaid did not move. Even if it hadn't been a still night he would have heard the gun being cocked.

Ambrose spoke once more. 'I ain't going to say it again. *Walk toward me!'*

Kinkaid looked northward. Ambrose noisily resettled the gun. Kinkaid started walking in the direction of the cabin where the dying candle was flickering in its bowl.

Ambrose stepped sideways to fling open the door at the same time he grounded the rifle and fisted his hawgleg. But Kinkaid did not enter. He was almost to the cabin when he abruptly hurled himself sideways, got against the front log wall and fired from the hip through the vacant window.

Ambrose kicked the rifle, which fell noisily and, outside, the man with the drooping feather yelled, 'Got the old one.'

Ambrose heard hurrying men coming from the north and east. They were also coming from behind the cabin westerly but stout log walls prevented him from hearing anything in that direction.

He crouched to flit past the open door, straightened up warily and waited. It was a short wait. The man with the droopy feather stepped clear of the wall as the other men called. He repeated what he'd said before. 'I got the old one!'

Ambrose leaned around the door and shot Kinkaid from a distance of less than twenty feet. The man with the feather threw out both arms as he fell backwards.

The sound of running men died after they had raced for cover in all directions.

For a long time there was not a sound, when it came it was the hoot of an owl behind the cabin somewhere and Ambrose swore. There was only one window, it was in the front wall; even the logs had been fitted so tightly there was very little chinking otherwise he might have been able to use his gun barrel to knock out chinking and see where that 'owl' was behind the cabin.

The silence ran on and Ambrose sweated even though it was chilly inside the cabin, and even colder outside where the man with the feather in his hat was spread-eagled in death.

A deep, venomous voice called out, 'You old bastard, we're goin' to roast you.'

Ambrose did not smell smoke for almost fifteen minutes, which was about as long as it would take men behind the cabin to get the logs burning. He had an agonising thought: he would never get to build another log house, but if he could have he'd put a window hole in every damned wall.

He could hear men talking without being able to distinguish words. They knew he was alone, that's why Kinkaid had broadly smiled. What they probably did not know was that George had escaped from the canyon. At least old Ambrose hoped with all his heart that was what had happened even though he had no illusions how this fight would end.

Staying alive, living and hoping, was important until

a man reached the age where aches spoiled it for him to watch the birth of each new day. After that, his wonder and pleasures gradually diminished and his main concern was—what came next. He did not necessarily fear it but he sure-Lord was curious about it.

Ambrose had been fatalistic most of his life, even when he had been younger. It was this fatalism that kept him calm now as the smoke-smell increased.

He went to the rear wall, put his hand against it, felt the heat, reloaded the single chamber that had been fired, picked up his long-gun and very carefully opened the door, expecting bullets to sluice inside but none did. However, he was not deluded. These were seasoned raiders, they rarely made mistakes. But this time one had, he was lying face up about twenty feet in front of the cabin door.

Ambrose listened and waited. As he had told George, he was not a praying man, nor did he pray now, his full attention was on the darkness and shadows beyond the doorway. They would be out there. It was the purpose of burning houses with people inside to shoot them when they were backgrounded by firelight.

Ambrose would not wait for that.

He did not consider the odds. He did not think about them at all. He wiped a sweaty palm, tried to guess where they were out yonder and ran for it.

The first shot broke a leg below the knee. He fired at the muzzle blast and tried to regain balance. The second shot came from directly in front, the direction he was going. It missed flesh but swung Ambrose off balance when it tore the sleeve of his coat on the left side. He fired in that direction too, twice as fast as he could cock and squeeze off the bullets. This time a man squawked, but Ambrose was still staggering in the same direction.

The shot that brought him down came from behind where men had rushed around to the front of the cabin.

Ambrose collapsed in a heap. A large, bearded man walked toward him from the direction of the cabin, stopped long enough for the old man to bare his teeth as they glared at each other, before the large, bearded man raised his arm slowly, cocked the six-gun and fired. Ambrose was punched in the dust under impact. He lost both his guns.

The large, bearded man methodically cocked and aimed one more time. Ambrose neither heard the gunshot nor felt the bullet.

Flames were licking up the rear of the smaller cabin as the large man called for his companions to rifle the large cabin and fire it too.

None of them went about their work in haste. They knew exactly how isolated Killian's canyon was. Even burning cabins in the night would be invisible if folks were asleep in other places and farther, down at Bridgerville.

One of the men, a young Indian with a knife-scarred face was disappointed that they had not got the horse. To this the large bearded man said, 'If you'd kept close watch like you was told to at the mouth of the canyon the other one wouldn't have got clear.'

Even the escape of the younger canyon dweller did not encourage haste among the plunderers. Wherever the man had gone on his pudding-footed big horse, he wouldn't reach a ranch or the town before dawn, which was why raids were made in darkness.

A raider with a slightly hunched back, close-set eyes and a bloodless slit of a mouth, found George Killian's ivory-handled straight razor, a parting gift from Killian's father when George had left Ireland.

They took everything they wanted, including blankets, cooking utensils; ammunition for the guns they did not find, and were ready to ride by the time the night-chill had become pre-dawn cold.

What they left was two gutted log houses, a dead old man who had five bullet holes in him. They took his guns. From his cabin one of them had also taken the wicked-bladed big knife the old man had used for skinning buffalo many years earlier. It had two initials burned in the smooth bone handle. A.W.

This close to daybreak the large bearded man led the withdrawal northward in the direction of the concealed camp far inside a forest of fir and pine trees.

They had the man who had said his name was Kinkaid tied belly-down across his horse. The only comment made concerning his passing was when a very dark man with a hairline only inches above his eyebrows said, 'Damn fool. He didn't shoot that old man.'

Another renegade rebutted that. 'He thought he did. I knew Walt better'n anyone else. He wouldn't have moved away from the front of the house if he hadn't believed he'd killed that old man.'

The discussion ended when the large, bearded man growled and pointed. He was sitting twisted in the saddle. Some coal oil Killian had stored for winter was putting up a large, oily black cloud which showed black against the dawning new day. As he straightened forward the large man said, 'I didn't see no oil cans.'

Whoever was responsible for allowing the black cloud to rise high enough to be seen for many miles, was prudently silent.

It was entirely possible none of them had deliberately fired the barrels, it was likely they had ignited of their own volition when the inside of the largest cabin had become engulfed in flames.

The large man tucked a cud of tobacco in one cheek and said, 'Well, it was time to move anyway.'

3

An Interlude

There were nine of them ranging in age from about twenty into much higher brackets. Mister Bullock, the general store proprietor, was in front when they reached the yard. He saw Ambrose about the same time Killian saw him. George kept riding. Mister Bullock threw out an arm to halt the others. They dismounted looking at the devastation but Mister Bullock watched George, who dismounted, stood briefly, then sank to one knee, crossed Ambrose's arms across his chest, dropped his hat, made the sign of the cross, bowed his head for about a minute then arose. Killian was a fearless man but not a vengeful one, but that changed as he counted the bullet wounds. It was never known whether he blamed himself for the old man's death but as he led his pudding-footed big combination horse back where the others stood, he asked the storekeeper if there was a man among those who responded to his shouts and gun-fire in the wee hours in Bridgerville who could read tracks.

It was late dawn. Every man among the town-riders could see in which direction the tracks went—north-ward. Mister Bullock who knew everyone in the coun-tryside nodded in the direction of an ageless, thin man with a prominent Adam's apple who had a marked, lazy drawl when he said, 'Ben can. He done it for the army years back.'

Ben slowly masticated while looking Killian straight in the eye, and spat aside. He did not speak but a 'breed standing with him said, 'Only man I ever seen who could track a fly across glass.'

Ben was tall, with too-long hair, hadn't shaved in days, and not once lowered his eyes nor spoke. But he barely nodded and barely smiled, without once missing the rhythm of his working jaws.

Killian was holding his hat in one hand. He dropped it on the back of his head and addressed the storekeeper. 'I don't like to ask you gents—but if you'd bury

Ambrose, an' if Ben'll ride with me, I'd like to get on their trail.'

The lanky man, an Arkansan, still said nothing but he turned, ran a thumb under the cinch, found it snug enough, rose up and settled over leather. He did something few men who lived in mountainous country did, his saddle boot was slung forward under the fender, not the best way to carry a saddle gun if a rider had to make a sharp right turn.

Otherwise the lanky man wore a full shell belt and an ancient Colt six-gun with not a shred of the original bluing left.

Bullock took Killian aside, over near the ashes of the smaller cabin and said, 'He's short-tempered, like all them Arkansans. He'll fight at the drop of a hat, an' in town he drinks too much, but I can tell you for a fact, if he cottons to a person they can't do no wrong.'

Killian listened to all this and interrupted to say, 'I can't pay him, Mister Bullock. I got no money now— didn't have much before.'

The hefty older man patted Killian's shoulder. 'I'll take care of that. Boy, you be sure'n come back. Myrtle will be waiting.'

As Killian went among the townsmen thanking them for responding to his call in Bridgerville, one man pressed a little under-and-over .41 caliber derringer into his hand. Another man, old and watery-eyed handed Killian a half-full bottle of Old Taylor.

He rode where Mister Bullock was standing, sat with both hands atop the saddlehorn in silence. Mister Bullock understood. 'We'll settle Ambrose right, don't worry. When you come back he'll have a decent headboard.'

Killian looked over where the lanky Arkansan was sitting his horse. Killian nodded. They left the others in the fire-scented new day without speaking to each other or looking back. If Killian had looked back he would have seen something unexpected. That 'breed Indian was following behind at a distance of about 200 feet.

Ben, nor anyone else had mentioned that the Arkansan and the 'breed shared the same tar-paper shack out behind Bridgerville; where one went the other followed. In a sense they were partners.

Ben only occasionally glanced at the ground. The tracks were too plentiful to require much attention. But when the trio was approaching the timbered uplands Ben stopped, handed Killian his reins, took his saddle gun and went ahead on foot. The 'breed rode up beside Killian. He said, 'My name's Jawn. J-a-w-n. Me'n him is partners.' The 'breed smiled, he was by nature an amiable individual who accepted what life handed him with no complaints. He also said, 'He'll find 'em. In '76 he was with the Crows at Little Bighorn . . . he got drunk, crawled into a cave to sleep it off, come out with the sun goin' down, found an In'ian horse and went back. . . . Missed the whole damn fight.'

Ben had disappeared in the timber. Killian and the 'breed dismounted. George asked if Ben had any other name, and the In'ian's face split into a wide grin. 'Percival. Ben Percival. But he don't use no name but Ben. An' somethin' else; he can shoot the eye out of a squirrel at thirty yards.'

Killian was impressed. 'That's good shooting,' he said, and the Indian broke into laughter as he also said, 'With the squirrel runnin'.'

Killian looked impassively at the other man and the Indian doubled over laughing. He was an incorrigible jokester.

During the wait for Ben's return Killian decided anything the 'breed said was at the very least, likely to bear only a remote association with the truth. And he was right.

Ben returned with the sun nearly overhead. He was carrying a small stick with which he pointed eastward, then dug for a fresh cud to tuck in his face. 'More'n ten raided you. Women with 'em. Crow In'ians. Renegades. They buried one up there. There's another one on a travois, shot I'd guess. Usually they don't take 'em along. Slows 'em down.' Ben spat. 'You want to keep goin'?'

Killian glanced skyward, the day was only half spent. He nodded. Without another word Ben mounted, winked at his friend the 'breed and led off.

The trail continued to meander through timber and a few small clearings going east, which was understandable, southward timber was scarce, open country predominated.

Twice Ben stopped, handed over the reins, took his short-gun and melted among trees and their shadows.

The 'breed grinned each time as he and Killian waited. He said, 'No bushwhack.'

By evening they had moved into country George Killian was only remotely familiar with. There were arroyos chock-full of undergrowth, trees tall enough for a man to have to lean all the way back to see their tops. They crossed two cold-water creeks and Ben halted at the third, led his horse to a clearing with grass, hobbled it, hauled his rig back beside the creek and said, 'You got any jerky, Mister Killian?'

George shook his head. Jawn produced two greasily wrapped bundles. One he gave to Ben, the other he unrolled to share with Killian.

Fortunately the creek was close by. Few things on earth made a man thirstier than jerky.

Ben produced that little stick he had brought back with him from his first scout. He drew lines in soft earth at the bank of the creek. 'Band's maybe half renegades, half Crows. They got women with 'em.'

George said, 'How many?'

'They buried the one they had on the travois up ahead in some rock half a mile or so. I got to guess; maybe sixteen, eighteen. Maybe more. Hard to tell when all the horses is bein' rode bunched up.' Ben put aside the little stick with berry-stain marks encircling it which he'd found on his first scout. 'Mister Killian there's three of us an' a hell of a lot of them.'

George considered the lanky, Arkansan. 'I'm obliged to you an' your friend . . . I'll go on alone.'

Ben considered that briefly while making squiggles

34

with the little stick. He raised his eyes to the 'breed. They considered each other impassively for a moment before Ben said. 'Mister Killian, you keep goin' an' you'll never see sundown. Not today but tomorrow.' He again exchanged glances with the motionless and impassive 'breed before finishing. 'We'd best saddle up. Keep goin' until we scent-up somethin'.'

George faintly frowned. 'Scent-up . . . ?'

'Renegades worry more about what's behind 'em than what's in front. They got to have eyes in the back of their heads. Bushwhack, Mister Killian, an' I'd say this bunch, bein' real savvy, on'y lived this long by watchin' their back-trails like hawks.'

From this point on they halted often. Not until the timber thinned did they consider halting and that only happened when they came upon another cold-water creek with the sun behind them and turning red.

Even Killian could read sign here; the Indians had halted to rest their animals, fill their water bags and the few US Army canteens and had then pushed on.

Ben swung down, led his horse across the creek, hobbled it before removing its saddle, bridle and blanket, which he carried back to the creek-side camp, dumped everything and looked at the 'breed who dumped his own riding equipment, then left the others without a word to scout up stream.

Ben tossed down his hat, vigorously scratched inside his shirt and got comfortable and skived off a chew which he pouched into a cheek. He gazed in silence eastward for a long time before addressing

Killian. 'It ain't right what they're doin'.'

'Going eastward?'

'No. Not leavin' a buck every mile or two to ambush us.'

Killian accepted that without comment. What he knew about renegades was from hearsay. He knew nothing at all about how they moved or their strategies.

Jawn returned wet to the knees and grinning from ear to ear with seven Dolly Varden trout, in their prime and plump. He had gutted them where he had snared them. Without a word Ben used his belt-knife to dig a hole. When it satisfied him he mounded the cast-aside soil around the hole, Jawn brought deadfall twigs which would burn fiercely without smoking, and they built a tiny fire at the bottom of the hole. Jawn cooked the gutted fish using latticed green twigs. While he was doing this Ben wandered eastward past the hobbled animals and out of sight in the yonder timber.

Killian said, 'He's uneasy,' and the amiable 'breed shook his head. 'He goes far out to see if watchers can see our fire.'

When the fish were cooked they first killed the fire by scuffing dirt into the hole, then ate four of the seven trout. The other three they would eat tomorrow, after sunrise wherever they stopped again and could build another fire which would not smoke.

Killian did not sleep well, particularly after the chill arrived. He did not know one of his companions was missing until his eyes were adjusted to the night.

Jawn's smashed-flat bed ground was empty. Closer,

the lump where Ben slept was discernible and when George sat up the Arkansan's drawl came out of the darkness with the kind of clarity only wide-awake people were capable of.

'Don't fret about Jawn. He can sneak right in among 'em an' slit five throats an' be gone before they know he's around.'

Killian asked if the renegades were that close, and Ben sighed. 'No; or they'd have lifted our hair by now, but by my calculations they ain't more'n three, four miles yonder.' Ben lay back. 'Go to sleep. Tomorrow we likely got a long way to go.'

That was true, the following day they rode past two camps left by the renegades, and just short of dusk they came upon a muddied creek where the renegades and their companions had rested and watered the horses not long before.

Before they came upon this place Ben did as he had been doing more often as they progressed; made a thorough scout of the area.

When he returned to get astride and lead his companions ahead he said something guttural and Jawn straightened up in his saddle, not smiling, more alert, but without placing the Winchester across his lap.

When they reached the abandoned camp Ben swung off, pointed northward and Jawn disappeared into the timber, this time carrying the saddle gun.

When he reappeared he was pulling and pushing an angry old woman who spat imprecations at him in some language Killian had never heard before.

Jawn pushed her to the ground. She looked from Killian to Ben and spat words at them, only two of which Jawn could interpret.

'Dina sica!'

Jawn said, 'She's not Crow, she's Lakota. She said this is no good.'

The people who had abandoned her had given her a buckskin bag of jerky, which was as greasy on the outside as it was on the inside. They took it from her, took what they needed and gave it back.

She was very old, very wrinkled, with the hooded eyes of a reptile. Her eyes were black, her hair was straggly and mostly grey. Ben pointed in her direction with a stick of jerky. 'Older'n Gawd,' he said, chewing. 'You see a grey-headed In'ian, Mister Killian, they're real old.'

The old woman chewed jerky with them, reached for Killian's canteen and drank it nearly empty. Then she studied them individually, one at a time. When she had finished she addressed Jawn, whose brow wrinkled. He knew only a few Lakota words. Jawn was a half-breed southwestern Papago.

He shook his head and told her in southwestern Spanish he did not understand. She fixed him with a hostile stare, and swore. They all understood from her expression and the way she spat out the words she was displeased.

Ben tried English. He said, 'Why did they leave you behind?'

She spat at him too; she did not understand English.

George and Jawn exchanged a look. Killian rolled his eyes.

Jawn finally tried Spanish, the Mexican variety, and the old woman fiercely shook her head.

Ben finished eating, went to the creek to refill Killian's canteen, drink and wash off the grease. When he returned he sat down, dispassionately looked at the old Sioux and said, 'Y'see how big that jerky bag is? Well, they give 'em plenty food an' water when they leave 'em to die. That's about what they done with her. She's a burden on 'em.'

Killian asked an innocent question. 'Then why'd they bring her along in the first place?'

Before Ben could reply the old woman raised a rigid arm and pointed back the way they had come and said something which none of them understood. She then groped for two sticks, stuck one in the creek-side grass and placed the other one across it to form a Christian cross.

Killian nodded. 'That grave we found yesterday. . . .'

Ben finally understood. 'It was her buck, most likely her son.'

Killian held his hand like a cocked pistol to his chest. The old woman nodded as her shriveled lips quivered.

There was a brief, awkward silence before Ben pointed easterly. This time, while the old woman probably understood, she replied fiercely. She knew what he wanted to know—how far ahead was the band, and would not have told them if she could have.

Ben sighed. 'They buried her man back yonder, abandoned her, an' wild horses couldn't drag it out of her where the band's heading.'

That did not surprise George Killian, the old woman had impressed him from the beginning as being defiant. He asked Ben what they should do with her. The Arkansan's answer was straightforward. 'Leave her.'

'How far would she have to go to get back to her people?'

Jaw and Ben exchanged a look. Jawn shrugged. 'Many miles.'

'On foot?'

Jawn shrugged about that too. 'She don't have no horse.'

'Look at her moccasins, they're worn through.'

This time Ben spoke. 'She heard me, went scuttlin' into the timber. I caught sight of her, let her think I hadn't an' rode back. When we got here I told Jawn about where he'd find her. Mister Killian, she ain't our concern.'

George frowned. 'How long a walk back to her tribe, Ben?'

'Maybe two, three months—if a cougar or somethin' don't get her. Or the army.'

'In those moccasins?'

Ben did not look at the old woman's footwear, he looked at Killian. 'What do you want to do with her?'

The old woman was gently rocking back and forth looking straight ahead past her captors, in fact past everything of this world. She only occasionally made a slight whimpering sound.

It required no particular knowledge of Indians for Killian to understand. He had gone to funerals in Ireland, only there the women cried aloud and wept. At his grandmother's funeral . . . the first he'd attended, the impression never left him. The old Sioux was about the same age. He asked Ben how many actual miles and the Arkansan made a rough guess.

'Maybe three, four hunnerd—if her people are still up there. These days with soldiers huntin' 'em an' drivin' them to reservations, maybe she'd never find 'em.'

Ben filled his mouth with jerky, looked at the Papago, they exchanged an impassive look before Ben went after another drink at the spring. This time when he returned and sat down he spoke bluntly. 'I don't expect she'd ever make it . . . she's too old . . . it'd be a favor to shoot her.'

Killian's eyes widened, which Ben did not see, he was rhythmically chewing jerky. Jawn spoke up. 'They might hear the shot, Ben.'

The Arkansan sat chewing and gazing at the old woman. He abruptly arose to go find a bedding ground. After he had departed Killian told Jawn, 'We can't do that.'

'She's too old,' the 'breed replied as though they were discussing a lame horse or an old dog. 'It'd be best for her. She could maybe find her son or whoever got buried back yonder.'

Jawn arose to go out among the horses before also seeking a place to bed down. Night was approaching, and this night there would be no little fire. It wasn't needed for jerky.

Killian sat watching the old woman for a long time before trying to communicate with her. It was a complete failure. She not only did not understand him she would not look at him; she no longer made a sound but she still rocked back and forth.

Killian remembered his grandmother. She hadn't rocked but she had sat in a chair near the hearth with a howling Irish wind outside, doing exactly what this old Indian woman was doing—looking far off, far away. He remembered her like that now. He also remembered creeping back to bed, and in the morning watching another old woman dress his grandmother in her one fine black dress. She had died in front of the fire sometime during the night.

He offered the old woman a stick of jerky. She did not see him. He held out a canteen. She did not see that either, but some time later she crept back toward the timber to find a bedding ground, and this time, because it was a totally silent, star-washed night, he could hear her crying.

Killian didn't sleep. When Jawn and Ben arose to stamp their feet for warmth he was still sitting where they had left him. Jawn would have approached but Ben flung out a sinewy arm and shook his head.

They went to the creek to wash and drink, and afterwards to seek the old woman's parfleche and help themselves to jerky. That was what brought Killian out of his reverie. He watched them and said, 'Three or four hundred miles in worn out moccasins—an' us eating most of the jerky they left for her . . . ?'

He arose, went to the creek, splashed cold water into his face and returned. Ben and Jawn were standing like rocks looking at him. Behind him the old woman came soundlessly, stepped past for some jerky and hefted the parfleche, which was considerably lighter than it had been, but she said nothing, only slung it from a bony shoulder, looked at the whitemen and the 'breed, and said something which for once hadn't sounded like swearing. She even made a little *wibluta* sign which only one of them understood and which signified goodbye.

Ben and Jawn continued to stand like rocks watching Killian, who let the old woman get a few yards away, then called to her. She turned. Killian touched his chest. 'George,' he said, pronouncing it carefully.

She repeated it. 'Gee-org,' and touched her own chest speaking a name that seemed to be made up of about five or six words.

George did not attempt to repeat it. He thought of another old woman thousands of miles away and long ago. He said, 'Kathleen,' smiled and pointed to the old woman. For a moment or two she formed the name with her lips before saying, 'Catlin?'

George nodded. That had been his mother's name. 'Catlin, you come with us?'

Neither Ben nor Jawn moved nor spoke. The old woman looked from them to George. Ben raised one hand sideways, used the first two fingers of the other hand to straddle the edgewise hand, and jerked his head.

The old woman's black eyes swung back to George. She again said something the men did not understand, but this time she repeated Ben's *wibluta* sign and also pointed a finger at George and made a sweeping gesture.

George made a guess and nodded.

The old woman walked back to them, an odd look in her very dark eyes.

Ben and Jawn gazed at one another. Neither spoke, rolled their eyes or regarded George and the old woman; they both turned to go bring the horses.

4

Action!

Ben did not say ten words all morning and, except to hand over his reins, take his carbine and scout on foot, he seemed almost detached.

About noon with heat rising he returned from a scout, spoke aside to Jawn, who left them following Ben's tracks like a bird dog, carrying his Winchester in one hand at his side.

While the others waited Ben pouched a cud, spat once and while gazing in the direction Jawn had taken, he spoke casually to Killian without looking at him. 'Bushwhackin' In'ian.'

The old woman, who had ridden behind Killian was expressionless. She knew—had to know—what was happening. Without the faintest idea what the lanky, taciturn man had said, she watched intently for Jawn's return.

It was a long wait. They sought shade, slipped bridles, let the hobbled animals pick grass and did not speak until Jawn appeared like a wraith, not from the easterly direction he had taken when he'd left, but down a northerly slope where timber was thick.

Ben turned in that direction, motionless and silent, not even masticating until he saw Jawn, then he spat aside and made a grunting sound which brought the old woman's head swiftly around. She too saw the 'breed emerge from forest shadows, but all she did was sit down and wait.

Jawn was sweaty and thirsty. First he tanked up from a canteen, then he ignored George and addressed Ben. 'You was right. He was settin' atop a rock, listenin' . . . young buck.'

Ben ignored all that. 'You got him?'

Jawn patted the sheathed knife on the left side of his shell belt. 'He jumped like a goat. He was watchin' the wrong direction.'

'Where's his gun?'

Jawn shook his head. 'Old army carbine. Older'n me. No good.'

From this point on they led the horses. Ben left them often and each time he returned they continued to lead the horses. By midday when Ben addressed George for

45

the only time thus far all he said was, 'Gettin' close.'

Killian did not have to be told that. He asked if the renegades wouldn't miss the Indian Jawn had killed. Ben was indifferent. 'I reckon, but scouts need lots of time. Maybe not until tonight.'

George accepted that. Every time Ben or the 'breed scouted they had an interim of waiting which was longer sometimes than at other times.

When they struck out, still leading the horses, the old woman satisfied Killian on one point: She had legs of sinew and muscle. Old though she was, she could keep up with any of them, and if the facts were known, she could out-walk a horse. She had done it many times.

Once she hung back to pick ripe berries the men had not noticed. She put them into the greasy jerky bag.

By late afternoon Ben and the 'breed exchanged opinions which resulted in an early camp at the first water they encountered. The animals were pleased about that. So was George although he wanted to get this over as quickly as possible.

The old woman acted from lifelong habit, she hunted for dry twigs, climbed a hill looking eastward, saw nothing and robbed four birds' nests on her way back. Ben did not make a fire hole. He told George they were too close, the renegades did not have to see fire if they could smell smoke.

The old woman made a hole in a bird's egg and sucked the shell dry. Killian watched in horror. She smiled at him as she repeated the process two more times.

46

Ben too sucked an egg, but Jawn rifled the greasy sack instead. He and Killian ate jerky. As Killian watched—and listened to the egg-suckers—he felt slightly nauseous.

Jawn wiped his face on a filthy cuff and smiled. He had seen that expression on other whiteskins many times.

Ben left them just ahead of sundown carrying his Winchester. The old woman watched his departure and muttered something neither Jawn nor George understood, then she poured water from one of the canteens over her hands, sluiced her face, and produced a thin-bladed long knife from somewhere among her clothing and used its sharp tip to slide bits of jerky from between her teeth.

George looked away. He was gradually being forced to change his opinion of two old women—his grandmother and the old Lakota. Maybe they shared some characteristics, but they did not share many.

They made a fire-less dry camp. The grazing horses made more noise than the men made. Even Catlin sat in stony-faced silence.

Ben eventually walked back, out into the night, but westward, not in the direction of the fleeing renegades. He was not gone long and after he returned Jawn did the same thing.

By this time what was left in Catlin's jerky sack was precious little.

George passed time trying to talk to her. The old woman with the sharp black eyes listened, repeated words but despite her best efforts few words came out understandably. When Ben returned from a scout and watched, he finally said, 'She's spoke Lakota too long,' which was the truth, but George persisted from time to time and Catlin tried. She picked up two words, not from George, from Jawn. She pronounced them almost perfectly: 'Son bitch.'

The following day when Ben led out he only rode a short distance before dismounting and gestured for the others to do the same.

By early evening when the old woman was walking with her head down to avoid sharp rocks, Jawn abruptly stopped, raised his head, said 'Smoke', to Ben, who left them among the big trees but was not gone long this time. When he returned he told Killian the renegades were camped on a bluff below which was a sprawling set of log buildings. 'Cow outfit,' he said. 'They'll hit it like they done your place—some time before sunup when the moon's gone.'

Jawn asked if Ben had got a count. The Arkansan shook his head. 'More'n we can handle,' and turned his attention to Killian. 'If we come in behind 'em it's got to be after the moon's gone.'

George frowned. 'Three of us?'

Ben spat aside. 'After the raiders is gone we could maybe scatter the women an' some of their horses. It might not save them cowmen, but it sure would upset the raiders, especially if we fire guns on the bluff after they go down to hit the ranch.' Ben paused to jettison his cud before finishing what he had to say. 'Mister Killian, set raiders afoot an' you got 'em two-thirds broke to lead. Them folks among the log buildings would hear our gunshots. We can't do no better than to warn them like that—and play hell behind the raiders.'

Catlin, who was hunkering close to George, followed every word that was being said. She did not have to understand what was being said, all she had to figure out was that the men she was with knew where the Indians and renegades were, which was plain enough from the lanky man's expression.

She sat like a wizened animal, black eyes alive, face expressionless.

Killian did not disagree with the lanky man. Ben seemed to have been in things like this before. One thing George had learned was that the taciturn lanky man had no compunction about killing, and he was right, Ben didn't have, hadn't had since middle childhood when he'd learned from experience that one thing mattered—survival.

Killian's purpose in this affair was to find the men who had killed Ambrose, robbed him and burned his cabins. What Ben was doing, seemingly in his casual, off-hand way was teach Killian how to exact vengeance and do it in a way that would guarantee his own survival. Killian couldn't have had a better teacher.

Ben sat on the ground, ignored the old woman, got a fresh cud in his cheek and spoke quietly in his drawling way. 'When I was a kid, I seen what renegades done to friends of our family—strung their insides over the bushes, an' that wasn't the worst they done . . . Mister

Killian, I hate raiders like them we're trackin' more'n anythin' else on earth, that's why I come with you. In'ians is bad enough, but renegades. . . .' Ben stopped to expectorate and wag his head. 'Ambrose got off lucky, they shot him all to hell. Now, I got to look around a little. They sure as hell got scouts out this time. They can't have no one behind 'em. Not this time.'

After Ben departed, Killian turned to the 'breed. Jawn said, 'He goes after them kind any time he hears they're around. He told you part of why he hates 'em. I'll go with him when he's ready.'

George fished forth the little under-and-over belly-gun a man had given him back in his yard. The thing was loaded. It was a large calibre for such a small weapon. Jawn eyed it and said, 'Kick like a mule.'

When Ben returned the night was turning cool. He brought something with him, a rump of cold venison which had probably been cooked the last time the rene-gades had made a fire.

George fed some to Catlin. The four of them ate the entire haunch. Afterwards Ben told them he had found a cache to the rear of the bluff, had waited hidden in leaves until two garrulous women had taken what they had wanted and left, after which he stole the meat.

He also said there were not many men at the camp; he thought their leader, that large, bearded man had already sent scouts to study the log buildings. Ben winked at Jawn. 'When they make their first run on the ranch, we'll fire behind them on the bluff. Them folks down there got to hear us. That's the best we can do for 'em.'

Killian had a question. 'How many men will be left in the camp?'

Ben shrugged. 'It don't matter if we can scare the whey out of 'em. For all they know we're the army. They'll run like the devil's after 'em.'

Killian thought that indeed, the devil was after them, and he was sitting across from George wearing a lively expression.

Catlin brushed Killian's sleeve. She offered him her thin-bladed knife. Jawn grinned. 'She's goin' to substitute you for the man she lost. They don't make presents of somethin' like that. They can't get another one very easy.'

When George hesitated Ben said, 'Take it.'

Killian accepted the knife, patted the old woman's arm and was turning away when she said something incomprehensible except for the tone of her voice. Jawn chuckled but Ben didn't. He said, 'Shove the knife inside your boot.'

In the darkening distance a wolf sounded. Moments later there was an answer. Ben shook his head at the 'breed indicating that he was satisfied it had been wolves not Indians imitating wolves.

Ben was restless. For one thing they were no more than a mile west of the bluff. For another thing he knew very well that renegades did not attack until they were satisfied it was safe to do so, which meant scouts in all directions.

He left their forested place pacing soundlessly in a south-easterly direction. Jawn watched the lanky man disappear before saying, 'In'ian don't learn good. In'ian don't sneak up on white man more'n white man sneak up on In'ian.'

One of their tethered mounts suddenly threw up its head. George called Jawn and pointed. The 'breed did not move, did not even seem to breathe. Catlin was as still as a stone watching the area in which the horse was looking.

The other horses raised their heads, ears forward, looking intently north-easterly.

When Killian looked around the old woman was gone. Jawn was only momentarily surprised, then arose, quartered and also moved silently away.

If heritage had anything to do with it a man born in Ireland with only a cursory acquaintanceship with an untamed, wild, raw world, should have reacted with something close to fear. But maybe heritage required centuries not generations; Killian moved toward the nearest trees, leaned beside a rough-barked old red fir and waited, alert to every sound, every whisper.

That someone had discovered them he had no doubt, nor was he surprised. Ben had said renegades scouted in all directions.

How Catlin had managed to disappear without a sound while sitting next to him was not incomprehensible; anyone who had lived as long as she had in an unpredictable and deadly environment would react as she had reacted.

He moved slightly around the old red fir. Something struck the tree above where his head had been. The sound was muted but the shock of the striking object made Killian crouch, slide farther around the tree. Because his eyes were adjusted to the gloom the hurtling figure with the upraised knife for silent killing was in view for fifteen feet before it reached the tree.

Instinct as old as time guided Killian's reaction. He did not wait, he spun around in the figure's path and sprang ahead.

They came together five feet west of the tree with the wraith slashing downward. Killian blocked the knife with an upraised forearm. The blade cut through his coat and shirt. There was a scratch but he was unaware of it.

The man grunted, struggled to raise the knife arm and Killian, with no time to use his belt-gun, struck with a rock-hard fist.

The man faltered for several seconds then would have back-pedalled but Killian, with the initiative, kept it, pushed the fight with flailing fists.

It was an Indian who showed no expression. His knife arm started a lunge. Killian swung sideways as the Indian sprang. The blade barely cut cloth. Killian raised his right fist as the Indian went past, struck the man hard under the ear. The man fell like a stone, his grip on the knife loosened.

Out of nowhere Catlin sprang upon the downed renegade with the fury of a catamount. She had no weapon. She was frail and old. She caught the unconscious

Indian by both ears and furiously beat his face against the ground.

Killian's attention was drawn to something else. He picked up the knife lying ahead of the Indian, turned it over, read the burned-in initials A.W. and was holding the knife when Ben materialized like a ghost, took the knife from George, tapped Catlin on the shoulder and handed her Ambrose's fleshing blade. She pulled back and threw herself forward with all the strength of her body. The knife buried itself to the hilt.

When she arose she said a name which the men did not understand. Clearly, she had known the renegade, and just as clearly killing him hadn't bothered her.

They moved among the trees. Twice Killian found an overhead opening in the treetop canopy where stars shone. They met Jawn near the horses. He had found no one in his scout. They told him what had happened. He grinned broadly at the old woman before saying, 'I went east. They're getting ready. It ain't that late, is it?'

Ben had no interest in the time, only that the attack was about to be made. He gestured for Jawn to lead them back the way he had come, got a fresh cud in his cheek and did not say another word until the 'breed halted behind a fringe of trees and pointed.

Some distance ahead, not distinct but discernible, men were readying horses. It seemed to George to be at least twelve, maybe even fourteen raiders getting ready.

Ben moved back to a dead-fall and sat on it. He showed no anxiety. Catlin talked excitedly, pointing out individual Indians until Ben growled her into silence.

Killian gave her back the knife she had presented to him. He had Ambrose's knife in his belt. Whether the buck Catlin had killed was the man who had killed Ambrose or not, the fact that he was carrying the knife fixed his fate with Killian—but it hadn't happened that way. Ambrose was dead when the buck found the knife.

Ben and Killian watched a large, bearded man mount a big powerful bay horse. Clearly, he was leader of the renegades. When he growled at someone they obeyed instantly.

Ben raised his Winchester. 'If he's head In'ian an' I can kill him before they start down—'

Two mounted Indians rode up to the bearded man. Ben lowered his weapon in monumental disgust. The Indians completely obscured his view.

Jawn moved slightly. To him the fact that everyone's attention was fixed on the raiders did not preclude the possibility of someone walking back and discovering them. Catlin punched Jawn with a bony elbow and said something sharp. Jawn stopped moving.

The bearded man sat like a carving until his companions were mounted, then made a slight gesture and went toward a game-trail leading from the bluff to the open grassland country below where the log buildings were barely visible by starlight.

Jawn looked at Ben, who shook his head. 'Not yet. Let 'em get down the trail.'

Schemes such as this one never went entirely as planned. An older Indian woman, stocky and very dark, had a food cache out a-ways. It was some hours before sunup and time to eat but she evidently was one of those souls who did not wait until the last minute to do things. She left the others watching the raiders depart, walked away from the camp, was some distance from it in fact when she came face to face with old Catlin.

The woman stopped stone still. Catlin was sitting on a dead-fall looking directly at the younger woman. She neither moved nor made a sound. Among the massive old over-ripe trees in star-dusted gloom, she was as near to a specter as the other woman would ever see. Other women would have fainted on the spot. This woman had never fainted in her life and did not faint now, she whirled and ran screaming toward the people still listening to the descending riders below the bluff-face, ran in among them yelling about the ghost of the old woman they had abandoned. When others tried to calm her, the woman gestured and cried out and finally sank down on the ground gently rocking back and forth with the other people forming a silent, impassive circle watching her.

Occasionally someone would throw a furtive look in the direction of the cache.

Ben arose to stand with Killian slightly wagging his head. 'In'ians got good spirits that helps folks. One of 'em just helped us.'

Ben drew his handgun, nodded at Jawn and Killian, and fired over the heads of the people standing around the woman who had seen a ghost.

The result was instantaneous and predictable. People

screamed and fled in three directions. The fourth direction was down the bluff-face where the raiders had reached flat country. They heard the commotion above and halted bunched up.

In the middle distance dogs barked.

Ben, Killian and the 'breed shot their weapons empty, the sound of screaming people grew fainter. Two men appeared with Spencer rifles. One of them shot at the last muzzleblasts from the westerly timber.

Killian, Ben and Jawn reloaded as quickly as they could. The second one of those riflemen sank to one knee; this man was no haphazard shooter, he sought a target and got one when Ben leaned down to examine the cylinder of his handgun. Ben's hat arose into the air, bounced off a tree and flew away with the list of a wounded bird.

Ben did not raise up. He aimed his weapon, held his breath and fired back. One of the men with Spencer rifles did not fall, he pitched forward like a pole-axed steer.

His companion fled.

Loose animals ran in panic, several ran down the game-trail to flat country, shied wildly around the bunched raiders and raced into—and out of—the yard where those log buildings stood. Dogs barked furiously and two unsteady lights showed, one in the large mainhouse, another in a square building with an overhang and a porch, which was the bunkhouse for hired riders.

The bedlam did not diminish for roughly a quarter of

an hour but most of the yelling stopped earlier. As Ben said, renegades did not advertise their presence.

Several people crept back to catch horses. They were not altogether successful, if one horse stampedes, particularly in the night, they all stampede.

Killian correctly surmised there would be furtive activity until daylight. The rout of the renegades had been so precipitous they had left behind more than food and iron pots, they had also left behind things necessary for survival such as blankets, fire sticks, clothing, weapons and horses.

Before the bedlam on the bluff had entirely subsided there were gunshots down below. The advantage of surprise had been lost when Killian and his companions had kept up a rattling fire from atop the bluff.

He and Ben went through the timber until they could see below. Visibility was poor but muzzle-blast flames were visible from the buildings and elsewhere around the yard where the raiders had got on foot.

Killian tried to count gunshots from the buildings and failed. Ben thought there were at least six shooters down there, and maybe more. However many there were, he said with a grim smile, it would be enough to rout the renegades whose protection was good as long as they hid among the buildings, but not as good as the ranch's forted-up defenders.

Catlin came soundlessly to stand with Ben and Killian. She could not explain what else had stampeded the people, and in fact Killian would never know, but as she stood beside him, he grinned and winked.

Jawn appeared with a stalwart dark woman. He prodded her from behind with his six-gun. She was not young but she was attractive and totally expressionless until she saw Catlin, then her mouth fell open. Catlin spoke to her. The woman appeared unwilling to answer a dead person. Catlin spoke again, more harshly. This time the handsome woman replied. Ben nudged the old woman. She spoke to him but again, she might as well have spoken in Greek.

The handsome stalwart woman said, 'She told me who you are. That knife with letters on it belonged to my man. She told me she killed him . . . is that true?'

Killian was too surprised to find that the woman not only spoke English but did so with no accent that he stood staring.

Ben answered her. 'He's dead . . . who are you?'

'Elena Gardia. I am not Indian. I am Mexican. I went with my man wherever he went.'

Killian had a question. 'Who is the man with the beard?'

'Hendry Pickett—*el jefe*. The leader.'

Jawn spoke in a whisper to the Arkansan who was looking at the woman when he shrugged and said, 'If you want her, Jawn, but I'll tell you one thing about the likes of her . . . she'll pour molten lead from a bullet mould in your ear some night when you're asleep. I've known it to happen.'

5

Tracking

What kept the fight among the log buildings going after the advantage of surprise had been destroyed, was the doggedness of Hendry Pickett, but as time passed with no raiders being able to get inside buildings the futility of the attack became clear.

Below the bluff-winking muzzle blasts, an occasional shout, and the deeper sound of rifles over handguns did not begin to slacken off for almost an hour, by which time Jawn had tired of watching, had gone among the abandoned packs to find several hand weapons, four elegant gold pocket watches complete with chains, some money, but not much, and an Indian hiding among the packs. Their meeting was sudden. The Indian struggled clear of his protective *alforjas* and would have raised his hands but Jawn shot him. That was the only shot fired in the camp after its people had fled into the night.

Catlin jerked Killian's sleeve and led him away from the bluff to the camp where everything had been abandoned in haste.

She showed him a painted, circular bullhide shield and an eight-foot lance, both in front of a hide-covered small dome of a house. She touched the shield, stood looking at the lance, and muttered something. When an old woman came along, cringing and speaking in a pleading tone, Catlin told her who Gee-org was, that she would not be harmed and the old woman broke into tears, not a common occurrence among her people but not unheard of either.

If there were others skulking beyond the camp in darkness they did not appear. George had no idea why Catlin had taken him to the place where the shield and lance stood until Jawn came along, interrupting his profitable plundering to tell Killian the lance and shield had belonged to the old woman's son. What bothered Catlin was that one of the white renegades had appropriated the shield and lance and had placed them in front of his hide house, an Indian custom.

Jawn said, 'If she finds him she'll kill him. The custom is to bury the war shield and lance with the dead man, or to burn it. No one can take another man's thunder.'

The firing continued for about an hour. It ended suddenly. Down below, the defenders, with nothing to aim at, called out, their shouts clearly distinguishable as distant as the top of the bluff.

They were profane, defiant and challenging shouts. There were no answers. Where Ben was standing on the bluff he raised an arm tracking the sound of running horses below. When Killian returned he said, 'I'll send Jawn back for the horses. We scattered them sons of bitches like leaves. They couldn't come back up here.' Ben paused, head cocked listening. 'They ain't ridin' together. I expect we spooked 'em real bad.' He paused to consider Killian. 'We don't know which one killed your friend. We can find out but we got to catch at least one of 'em first.'

Killian understood the innuendo and answered it without hesitation. 'Send Jawn for the horses.'

Ben did not move. 'Leave your old woman here. She'll find some others.'

'Ben, she killed one of them. The others will kill her for that, won't they?'

The lanky man nodded bleakly. 'All right, but we got to catch her a horse.'

Catlin did that with no knowledge of the conversation between Killian and the Arkansan. She led the animal up to George by a horsehair rope, and smiled. He could not ask how she had found and caught the animal. With the 'breed not around they could smile at each other until that handsome, dark woman appeared. She said she had helped Catlin corner the animal where an arroyo had three steep sides.

Ben considered the handsome woman. His interest in females was minimal. He was a loner, an individualist, one of those frontiersmen who were annoyed by most women—most men too if the fact had been known.

She smiled at him. Ben abruptly turned at the sound of horses. Jawn rode up riding one, leading the others. When he saw Catlin's horse he shook his head. The old woman was scrawny, skinny, tough as rawhide and evidently very resourceful. Jawn did not mention the horse but he had encountered three men, one renegade and two Indians near where they had left their animals.

When he had yelled 'Here are some we missed, fellers' the renegades fled and Jawn brought back the animals.

There was a distinct chill in the night. Ben removed his old coat from behind the cantle, shrugged into it and considered Jawn owlishly. The 'breed had brought back three horses, Catlin had one, the handsome woman had none. Jawn correctly interpreted his partner's expression and said, 'I can take her along but I don't need no lead poured into my ear.'

Killian followed Ben down the game trail. He expected the Arkansan to ride into the yard where the log houses were, but at the base of the bluff Ben skirted wide around the buildings with Jawn on his left side. They spoke so quietly Killian could not distinguish words. Only once did Ben turn. He watched Killian for a moment before speaking. 'Come dawn we'll track 'em', sat forward and did not speak again until it was close to daylight when Jawn rode ahead like a hunting dog, then Ben turned once more. 'Some are runnin' together.'

Killian said nothing. He knew the direction Jawn was taking them. Toward Bridgerville. He doubted that the fleeing renegades would enter the town and was correct, they wouldn't.

Catlin rode wrapped in an ancient, frayed blanket. In poor light she reminded Killian of pictures he'd seen as a child of witches. Every time their eyes met she smiled. She had a slight bulge in the front of her blanket. She had found a loaded six-gun at the hastily abandoned camp back yonder.

When daylight arrived Jawn held to the direction of Bridgerville. Ben dropped back to ride stirrup with Killian. He wagged his head. 'They got to change direction soon, unless they're crazy. Them fellers in Bridgerville who buried your friend won't take kindly to no broncos or whites dressed in buckskin.'

The trail veered north-easterly several miles above the town, which did not surprise Killian. Ben simply sighed. 'I know the country where they're headin'. They better get back north into the timber, ranches in the direction they're goin'.'

It was full daylight as they passed Bridgerville northerly where Jawn suddenly dismounted, scuffed some leaves and gestured to Ben and Killian.

The blood was fresh, not much of it but enough to indicate that one of the men they were chasing was bleeding. Ben thought the renegade had most likely been hit in the shoot-out at the log-house cattle outfit.

From this point on Jawn boosted his horse into a lope which Ben watched wearing a slight, tough smile. He told Killian when the 'breed was on a fresh trail he was like a coon dog.

Catlin ate from her greasy pouch. She hadn't overlooked plundering the renegade camp for food. In her life, next to staying alive, was food.

She offered Ben and Killian two strips of jerky, which they accepted. The jerky had been cured with as much pepper as salt. Killian made a guess about the Mexican woman having made it. Ben was indifferent about that, he watched Jawn ranging well ahead and eventually spoke around a mouthful of jerky. 'Danged fool, he's rode right past ten places where they could have shot him out of the saddle.'

The reason this had not happened was clear to Jawn up ahead. He could see tracks left by the fleeing renegades far ahead. The ground wasn't soft as much as it was dusty and over-grazed to bare earth. It took tracks like a blotter.

Ben only occasionally watched the ground. He was more concerned with the countryside they were passing through. Catlin made a guttural sound that made Ben pull to a dead halt. The old woman jutted her chin, Indian fashion. There was thin grey smoke, rising in the distance. Killian guessed it to be about two, maybe three miles onward.

Ben resumed riding but from here on he loped, which was the easiest riding-gait and horses could keep it up over considerable distances. It was not a fast gait, some horses could trot as fast as other horses could lope, the difference was that rangemen as well as frontiersmen never trotted if they could lope. Trotting was hard on the back, the kidneys, and other parts. It was also uncomfortable, particularly if a person was riding a short-backed animal. The hardest riding trotting animals were mules. They had backbones as inflexible as steel.

Jawn pulled down to a halt on a slight roll of land and sat up there like a statue until the others came up, then he pointed without speaking.

The fire had engulfed a solitary log cabin in the

65

middle distance. Ben said one word, 'Homesteader,' and led off in a lope down the far side of the land-swell to flat ground. Jawn called to him that the tracks led straight to that cabin. Ben's lips flattened. He did not take his eyes off the burning house as he approached it. Jawn called a warning but Ben ignored it. He rode with a six-gun in his lap. Killian got the impression that Ben, the renegade-hater, wanted someone to fire at him, but no one did.

They could not get close because of heat but that was unnecessary. The first thing they encountered was an old collie dog that had been shot. Beyond that was a rawboned large man standing above the sprawled body of a woman. She too was dead.

The man seemed unaware of approaching riders. They rode up and stopped. The man raised narrowed eyes in a sweat-streaked face. He neither moved nor spoke, stood looking at them as though he could see through them and beyond.

Killian swung down. The man allowed him to get within a few feet of the dead woman then raised his rifle and cocked it. George halted. Behind him Ben called to the homesteader. 'How long they been gone?'

The man shifted his attention to the Arkansan without speaking. Ben called to Killian, 'Get back astride.'

They left the man where they had encountered him. As they loped away he did not even seem to hear them. From this point on Ben took the lead. He did not slacken from a lope and he rode watching the ground.

Farther back Jawn spoke to Killian. 'He's goin' to kill the first man he sees.'

There was no mistaking the change in the Arkansan's bearing. He no longer rode slouched.

The trail veered slightly northward, away from the open grassland in the direction of forested hills. Catlin chewed jerky. Probably with having no idea of it, she had caught the horse of one of the renegades, a strong, ugly animal with little pig eyes and more "bottom" than most other horses. He kept up easily and with only barely breaking a sweat even after morning turned to afternoon.

Killian glanced back a couple of times. Catlin smiled at him. He thought those two, that ugly, tireless horse and the tireless old woman made a perfect team, and he was right.

They encountered four rangemen in mid-afternoon. One was a bushy-bearded bear of man with small eyes and chewing tobacco stains around his bearded mouth. Ben scarcely spoke. Killian explained who they were and why they were tracking. The bear of a man said one of his riders had been shot—not bad, in the arm—when he came upon a redskin and two outlaw-looking men stealing fresh horses on his range. He intended to hunt them down and hang the lot.

Ben spoke curtly. 'This is our business, mister. You do what you want but don't get in our way. We'll run 'em down all the way to the gates of hell.'

The cowman squinted at Ben. 'Ain't you the feller from Bridgerville who run down rustlers last year?

Ain't your name Ben—somethin' or other?'

'Name's Ben,' the Arkansan replied tersely and did not say whether the rest of what the stockman had said was true or not. He jerked his head. The others followed in the same easy lope they had used since they had encountered the burnt homestead. The bearded man watched them go, turned to his riders and growled, 'We won't foller 'em. That scrawny feller's of a frame of mind to shoot anything right now that crosses him.'

One of the riders said, 'What about the horses, Mister Reardan?'

The bearded man answered shortly, 'We got plenty of horses. That feller'll run 'em down an' kill 'em as sure as night follers day.'

The rider who had spoken would have made another comment if his employer hadn't turned and gigged his horse. He would have said those manhunters were riding tired animals, the men who had stolen Reardan horses and wounded one of them were riding fresh horses.

The cowboy was right, several miles farther along the horses began to drag their hind feet. Still farther, with a set of buildings visible on the horizon, even Catlin's animal showed signs of weariness.

Killian said they should try for fresh animals at that distant ranch. Ben did not agree, in fact he said nothing, but when Killian, Jawn and the old woman turned in the direction of the ranch he followed.

They had to abandon the trail but they could pick it up with fresh horses under them. Ben growled at Jawn about the waste of time. Jawn did something he rarely did, he said, 'We get fresh horses or we end up doin' the trackin' on foot an' them bastards'll get away.'

The sun was sloping away from the meridian. Ben squinted upwards several times. He also looked in the direction those tracks had gone—toward the timbered foothills behind which were stair-stepped ridges going always higher until they became mountains.

Tracking in that country wouldn't be only more difficult than the tracking they had done, but rooting out renegades in high country mountains would be just about impossible.

Ben rode the full distance to that ranch looking as grim as death. He did not speak and only indifferently acknowledged his companions.

Killian thought he had come to understand the Arkansan over the last few days but evidently he hadn't. It was improbable, but some day George Killian might reach a conviction: what made a man like Ben a merciless killer was part heritage and part maturing in a world where there was right and there was wrong. Killing women—any kind anywhere—was wrong and it was incumbent on men like Ben to exact punishment for that—and other—clear and obvious wrongs.

6

The Long Halt

The ranch they encountered was owned by a hefty widow-woman in her fifties. While Killian explained to her who they were and what they were trying to do—for which they required fresh horses—Ben stood apart, silent and aloof.

The woman's gaze wandered often to Ben as she and Killian talked. In the end she sent two riders to fetch fresh animals, had saddle and bridles switched, refused George's offer to pay for the animals when he could, leaned on a fence watching the three men and the old woman ride away freshly mounted.

Her rangeboss, an older man, came to lean beside her in stony silence until she eventually straightened up off the fence and spoke.

'That tall one will do it, Jeff.'

The rangeboss nodded without speaking. They both turned away. On his way to the barn the older man wagged his head. He had lived long, had seen his share of killers. Whether there was justification or not—and he thought in this case there was—that lanky man was what, in his younger days, Indians had called a "bloody hand", someone who rode out and did not expect to return. A killer.

Jawn quartered until he found the sign, gestured to the

others and rode ahead watching the tracks. They were going in the direction of those forested uplands.

The day had worn along. There was still a sun but it was sinking and during that process it gradually acquired a reddish tint. The old woman squinted skyward and said something about that blood-red sun the others did not comprehend. Jawn might have, but he was half a mile ahead riding directly toward some low, broken foothills where a few valley oaks grew and also where they started up cud-chewing cattle lying in shade.

The cattle fled like deer, and were ignored, but to range cattle anyone riding close was to be feared and fled from.

Jawn halted a short distance from the boundary between grassland and timbered country.

When the others arrived he would have pointed out where the tracks went directly into the timber but Ben growled at him, 'Keep goin'.'

Jawn led the way among the first tiers of giant trees. Killian wondered about an ambush; the country they were now traversing was ideal for bushwhacking. He said nothing but he watched the Arkansan.

Ben seemed indifferent to danger, but that was an illusion. Without craning around he missed nothing, not even when they splashed across a small cold-water creek where he saw something even Jawn had missed. Blood and what seemed to be part of a shirt-tail which had probably been a bandage which had been hastily hidden with dirt scuffed over it. It was fresh, moist earth that caught the Arkansan's attention. He dismounted, brushed soil and leaves aside, uncovered the bloody rag and remained on one knee for a long moment before speaking. 'That ain't cloth off an In'ian, so I expect the feller leakin' blood is a white. Somethin' else; that cloth was sticky . . . they ain't too far ahead.' Killian finally mentioned ambushing. Ben ignored George and spoke to the 'breed. 'I'd guess, all that open country we passed over—they always mind their back-trail.'

The 'breed inclined his head without his usual, seemingly automatic smile. Men who had partnered did not require a full explanation, and Jawn's interpretation of the Arkansan's unfinished comment was correct: the renegades knew they were being followed.

Ben sat his horse studying the territory. Every big old tree could hide a man, every brushy arroyo also could, as well as the age-old shadowy gloom they would ride through.

By now the renegades knew whoever was following them could read sign and with no way to avoid leaving tracks even in forested country where layers of pine and fir needles not only muffled sound but to a considerable extent did not take imprints well, the proof that experienced men were tracking them meant they either had to completely elude the trackers, or ambush them.

Ben shrewdly said, 'It's goin' to be horse against horse, unless they can find a creek. Water don't take tracks.'

Catlin was eating something when she slid to the ground, put her back to the others and went ahead in a crouch, for all the world resembling an ancient gnome.

Jawn and Ben watched her. Each time she stepped on a stone hidden by needles she flinched. Killian told himself that the first opportunity he was going to find footwear for the old woman.

What he did not know was that years of wearing moccasins made the soles of people's feet almost as tough as rawhide.

Ben told Jawn the old woman was quartering to find places the renegades had been. Jawn nodded without speaking but Ben finally called to the old woman. When she came back he tried to tell her using *wibluta* that all they wanted was the main trail.

She called him a name and went to her horse, mounted and glared. Killian almost smiled; Ben had belittled her and evidently she was as prickly about something like that as most whites would have been.

She did not offer to read sign again. Jawn led off but Ben sashayed on both sides of him, which might not have helped much if there were hidden bushwhackers, which apparently there weren't because they reached the first forested ridge without incident.

When they halted here, awed by the country ahead which could handily hide an entire regiment, Catlin got down again and, ignoring the 'breed and the Arkansan, resumed her erratic meandering, but this time she went down the far slope and stopped where a field of huge boulders required anyone riding in that direction to make a wide sashay around the rocks. She came back, paused to catch her breath and while looking up at

George made a *wibluta* sign which he did not understand, so she pantomimed by crouching, raising a hand to her brow as though shielding it from the sun, and turned her head from side to side.

Ben said, 'Them big rocks,' and dismounted. Jawn did the same. Killian was the last to dismount; he did it because clearly if the others were worried he also should be.

Jawn tried to talk to the old woman. She spoke back and although he did not understand Lakota he could pick out a word here and there. From this he told Ben the old woman had come upon those huge rocks from the east where trees were thickest.

Ben said, 'They down there?'

Jawn was cautious. 'Somethin' is. I don't know what she saw but she sure seen somethin'.'

Ben faced Catlin, but she was still smarting from their last encounter and turned her back on him. Ben turned to Killian. 'She's adopted you. See if you can talk to the old witch.'

George placed a hand on the old woman's shoulder. He did not say a word, he did not get the chance, she erupted in her language, jutting her jaw and even using an upraised arm in the direction of the rocks. She said her only two words of English, 'Son bitch' and stiffly pointed.

Ben walked over. The old woman went to her horse and kept her back to Ben. 'She saw something, Ben,' Killian stated. 'Maybe it was an animal, but whatever it is it's in those rocks. If it's a bushwhacker. . . .'

Ben nodded, went among the trees until he could see down the slope, then studied the trees and eventually began moving among them. Killian learned something else about the lanky man with the prominent Adam's apple: Ben could move like a ghost in forest gloom. Killian lost sight of him. Catlin came up and pulled Killian's sleeve, pointed rigidly and said something while holding one hand up and rigid with the fingers pressed together.

Jawn understood. 'It's a horse,' he told Killian. 'Down among them rocks is a horse.'

Jawn might have left the protection of the timbered ridge if Killian hadn't told him to stay where he was because a horse meant a rider.

It was a long wait. A man on a scout like Ben had no concern with time, only in creeping as close as possible, then doing the same during his withdrawal. By the time he got back to the timber shelter atop the ridge the sun had continued its inexorable descent.

Ben employed his customary routine of getting rid of one cud and cheeking a fresh one before speaking. His drawl was noticeable as he said, 'There's a hurt horse in a sort of hollow place among the rocks.' He paused before also saying, 'If there's a man down there he's hid real good.'

Killian made a suggestion which made Ben gaze at him in an almost pitying manner. He said, 'If they had to abandon a horse, one of them'll be carrying double. That should slow them down.'

Ben ruminated, looked down-slope beyond their

shield of trees and spoke dryly. 'Mister Killian, men like that don't ride double. If one of 'em gets set afoot, he's on his own. An' that worries me . . . we ride down there a-horseback an' if he's where he can see us, someone's goin' to get hurt.'

Ben offered no solution, he went after a canteen, drank and sought the 'breed. They hunkered in forest gloom. Catlin came up to Killian to tug at his sleeve. She raised two fingers to her lips, waited for understanding and when she saw none she spoke in Lakota gesturing with an upraised arm. When Killian still looked blank the old woman left him, went over to her horse, tied it securely—and disappeared. By the time Ben and Jawn had finished their palaver it was the lanky Arkansan who missed her.

He asked Killian, who had not known Catlin was gone until Ben brought his attention to the tethered bay horse.

Ben went back for another palaver with the 'breed. When they finished Jawn also tied his horse, but he was less adept at becoming invisible than Catlin was. Ben and Killian watched Jawn go among the trees. Ben said, 'Danged old woman. If he's down there an' sees her he'll shoot, and the fellers who left him will hear it.'

Killian asked if Jawn has gone to bring the old woman back and Ben shook his head. 'He went to see if he can draw the feller out—if he's hid down there. Mister Killian, we can't go past them rocks until we know.'

George rummaged Catlin's parfleche, withdrew two

sticks of jerky and no more because the food pouch was beginning to give off a sour odor.

Neither Catlin nor Jawn returned while the sun continued to sink. Ben was restless and irritable, when Killian suggested going a mile or two west of the boulders to continue the pursuit, Ben's retort was brusque. 'Mister Killian, if we done that an' there's one of 'em yonder in the rocks, we'd have him behind us an' we'd be settin' ducks.'

Catlin returned and glared at Ben. Neither of them understood what she said but the tone was unmistakably annoyed. Ben sighed. 'She seen Jawn as sure as hell. She's mad because she figured why he was tryin' to find her.'

Ben would have walked away but the old woman snarled and he turned. She squatted, cleared away needles and used a forefinger to draw what had to be large boulders, when she looked up they both nodded understanding. She drew a stick-man with her finger and looked up again. Ben said, 'There is one down there,' and sank to one knee as she used a finger outlining where the stick-man was. When he looked at the old woman he smiled and would have patted her hand but she pulled it away, arose, smiled at George and went over where the bay horse was dozing.

Ben stood up watching the old woman. 'Mister Killian, they're all the same. They don't forget, they carry a grudge.' He brightened. 'I got to say one thing in her favor, she can read sign better'n Jawn or just about anyone else. Look down there; the onliest way she could see into that place was if she climb a tree.'

Killian squinted skyward. 'It'll be light for another couple of hours . . . Ben, I'd like to go down there.'

The Arkansan's eyes sprang wide open. He had never been a tactful person, in his world there was no place for tact. 'Mister Killian, this ain't a game. You want to prove manhood like an In'ian—not here. It ain't so much that he'll likely kill you, that could happen to anyone, but his partners ain't so far off they wouldn't hear the gunshot.'

George replied doggedly. 'I want their blood as much as you do—maybe more. Old Ambrose was my partner. To tell you the truth I got a feelin' of guilt about leaving him.'

Ben was silent for a long moment then spoke again. 'Take the old witch with you. She'll teach you more in ten minutes than you'd learn on your own if you lived to a hunnert.' Ben saw Catlin watching them and gestured for her to join them.

She did, but ignored the Arkansan until he used *wibluta* to give her an idea of what he wanted her to do—go scout with Killian.

She brightened, brushed George's arm with her hand and led the way westerly until Ben could no longer see them. He smiled, sought shade of which there was an abundance, and was sitting on a crumbling deadfall when Jawn materialized sucking air like a fish out of water.

Jawn sank down and shook his head. 'Never seen her. Run out of tracks a hunnert feet from up here. She

78

must've dragged a blanket. One time there was sign, not real good but good enough. The next moment—no sign. I thought she clumb a tree an' looked, but never seen her up there.'

Ben listened patiently then explained that Catlin had not only returned with information about a renegade among the rocks, but had taken Killian with her to scout.

Jawn settled his tired body against the punky dead-fall. Ben handed him a canteen from which the 'breed drank before putting the canteen aside. *'Fantasma,'* he growled, and at Ben's puzzled look he said, 'Ghost. Where I come from that's what the Messicans call 'em. One minute you see 'em, next minute you don't.'

'She ain't no ghost, Jawn, she's an old squaw who's done maybe as much sign-readin' as you'n me put together.'

Jawn moved to get more comfortable. 'That feller she seen in the rocks—In'ian or white?'

'She didn't say. What difference does it make?'

'None . . . time's passin', Ben.'

'Nothin' we can do about that. Jawn, when we catch those sons of bitches I been thinkin', they'd ought to have fat money belts.'

Jawn nodded about that, he was by nature an invet-erate looter.

'Well, Jawn, you'n me is gettin' a little long in the tooth for this kind of work. . . .'

'Buy some land, Ben?'

'No. I put in about all the years I figure to doin' outside work. Buy a saloon. Maybe that one down in Bridgerville.' Ben looked down. 'We could stoke the fire in winter an' keep out of the wind in springtime, an' even keep cool when it got hot. What do you think?'

Jawn relaxed atop layers of fir needles—they were at too high an elevation for pine trees to thrive. 'Every now'n then,' he told the lanky man, 'you come up with a sound idea. I'll turn their pockets inside out an' if you're right, maybe when we get back we can do it.'

Somewhere down the slope a number of rocks rattled and rolled. Jawn groaned. 'Danged careless old woman.'

Ben said nothing, he arose, went among the final fringe of forest giants to look downward.

There was no movement, no activity at all. He hunkered. Anything could have set those rocks to tumbling but it would be stretching the probability of coincidence to the very limits to think it was an accident or that two-legged creatures had not caused the racket.

Jawn came over and dropped down. He had his saddle gun. Ben got a cud into his cheek, spat at a passing lizard and sighed. 'That bastard in the rocks sure didn't do that.'

Jawn agreed. 'No—why'n hell did you let Mister Killian go with her? He's got two left feet.'

Ben did not answer. Behind them a horse stamped. They both looked back. The old Lakota was standing beside her horse watching their backs. They arose, dusted off and walked back where she stood. Ben said, 'Killian?'

The old woman jutted her jaw northward which was down the slope. Jawn scowled at Catlin as he said, 'I told you—Mister Killian had no business scoutin' up a renegade—or a house cat for that matter.' Jawn tried to talk to Catlin. She listened, replied in her language and drew a stiff finger across her throat.

Jawn reacted. 'Ben—she got him killed!'

The Arkansan turned on his heel, walked directly toward the foremost screen of giant trees, paused only long enough to shift his Winchester from the crook of his arm to both hands, then did as he had done before when his blood was up, he stepped into clear sight and walked without haste in the direction of the boulders.

Behind him atop the slope Jawn flung out an arm to prevent the old woman from following Ben. She slapped the arm away, glared and walked past Jawn.

7

Big Timber

There was no gunshot. There was no sound of any kind. Ben was prepared to fire his saddle gun from the hip, lever up and keep firing. He sensed someone behind him but the closer he got to the boulders the more he resisted a fleeting look backwards. It wasn't Jawn so it had to be the old woman. The notion that she was following him caused annoyance but he was too close to the rocks to have his attention diverted, even for a moment.

There was a rifle pointing at him from a narrow slit between two man-high boulders. He concentrated on that; thus far it was the only danger he had encountered. Why whoever was behind that gun hadn't fired caused the Arkansan less anxiety than the fact that the gun in that notch among the rocks was pointing at him.

He did not stop walking, not even when the old woman closed the distance between them and growled something he did not understand. She hadn't warned him; she had made a suggestion. When he continued in the direction of the gun Catlin lengthened her stride, came abreast and said something in a sharp tone, tugged his sleeve and moved to her left.

Ben's temper flared. He flung off her hand, swore at her without looking away from the gun.

Catlin spoke the only words of English she had picked up, 'Son bitch!' and this time when she reached for his sleeve she gave him a rough tug. He could not avoid moving to the left. He flung her arm off again and swore at her.

The old woman could have been deaf. She ignored his anger to point. Ben looked, the gun was still pointing southward where he had been.

Understanding came slowly. He spoke softly, unconcerned that the old woman could not understand, then he moved toward the rocks from farther west with Catlin maintaining a distance of about fifteen feet between them, which had nothing to do with fear; she was following the age-old custom of women walking behind bucks.

The gun did not shift to Ben's new course. What she had told him after she'd pulled him sideways was that there was no one behind that gun. To test this notion when he got close to the nearest huge rock he sidled along it, flattened within arm's length, reached with his Winchester and raised it with great force to strike the gun. It rose up in its notch and noisily clattered down behind the rocks which had supported it.

Ben turned to Catlin. She said something and looked triumphantly at him. Catlin had triumphed over a seasoned frontiersman in a society, both redskin and whiteskin, which was male dominated.

She led off, pressing close to the rocks, produced that old six-gun from her clothing, held it at her side and did not look to see if the Arkansan was following. He was, but out a couple of feet from the rocks and with his Winchester cocked for swift use.

Catlin came to a place where the rocks were slightly less jumbled, paused to look once at her companion, then dropped flat, pushed her head around, had her view blocked by a stationary horse with a raw, bloody wound on its left flank. Ordinarily a horse would have known by scent there were stalkers nearby. This horse did not raise its head.

Catlin sought another place where the rocks had shattered and where she could see better, got belly down again, lay motionless for a full minute, then arose and without speaking continued to slip around the boulders until she found an opening. Here, she looked at Ben, faced inward and began soundlessly sidling among the boulders. He followed but not before raising the saddle gun.

Daylight was failing, inside the only clearing not obstructed by boulders, shadows were thickening. Ben followed the old woman until she halted peering around a shoulder-height rock. She stood motionless so long Ben elbowed her with impatience. She finally moved, and with nothing to obstruct Ben's view of the shadowy place ahead, he stopped stone-still for seconds, then swore aloud. Ahead in the little clearing George Killian was sitting beside an Indian attired in an old flannel shirt which did not match his buckskin britches or his moccasins. George had taken the precaution to toss a six-gun and a fleshing knife to one side. He looked up, saw Catlin first then Ben. He spoke to them in a normal, quiet voice.

'I don't know how he managed to get this far. He's shot through the body.'

The old woman reached them ahead of Ben, she looked at the Indian, leaned down to peel back his soggy shirt, considered the wound and said something in Lakota which the renegade answered in the same language. Catlin faced Ben, standing above the Indian with his cocked gun, shook her head and returned her attention to the Indian as Killian said, 'I came in from the north. He didn't see me. He was leaning against a rock making some kind of chant.'

Ben replied without a shred of compassion. 'His

84

death song,' and leaned to also consider the wound. The Indian said something to Catlin to which she gave a terse reply. He had asked if the tall man with the cocked gun was going to kill him. She had said it wouldn't be necessary and the Indian, a man in his early thirties, wanly smiled at the old woman.

She knew him but since Catlin and the white men could not converse she arose, walked over to the injured horse, examined its gaping flank, picked up some ancient dust and plastered it over the wound. The horse did not move.

Ben went over to her and used *wibluta* to indicate he wanted to know which way the other renegades had gone. She jutted her jaw northward and turned back to the injured horse.

Jawn came gingerly through the rocks. He too stood looking down at the injured renegade and like Ben, showed no compassion. He retrieved the discarded pistol and knife, examined the gun and flung it aside, the knife was old with a bone handle and a nicked blade. He also tossed that away before going back to the wounded man to kneel and make a rough search which turned up a buckskin pouch inside the Indian's bloody clothing, which he hefted and smiled at Ben as he said, 'Saloon money.'

Ben nodded, considered the Indian and shook his head. He told Killian the Indian would not be alive come morning and although evening was coming, they should be on their way. He said, 'This danged mongrel's held us up too long,' and turned to leave the rocks and hike uphill where the horses were tethered.

Jawn followed. Catlin did too but not until she had pulled weeds to pillow the renegade's head. Killian was the last to depart. He and the dying renegade gazed at each other for a moment before Killian leaned, made the sign of the cross on the Indian's chest, and said, 'May God be with you.'

The dying man, fully conscious, had not said a word to George. Now, he made a feeble gesture with one hand and spoke English.

'They go to Big Timber.'

George left the man, reached the top of the slope after the others were ready to ride and asked if Ben knew of a place called Big Timber.

The Arkansan nodded. 'He could talk English?'

Killian nodded as he went over to his horse, tested the cinch and was ready to ride when the others got astride.

They were threading their way through the field of boulders before the Arkansan spoke. 'There used to be a buffler hunters' camp up there. I been there a time or two. It's one hell of a distance.'

They threaded their way through the forested uplands, and for a change no one looked for a sign. Ben had a destination and the others followed.

They had been on the trail more than an hour before George looked back. There was no sign of Catlin. He called to Ben who halted, looked back and shrugged. Without a word he led out again.

Killian waited until they made a stop to rest the animals before worrying aloud about the old woman.

Ben's response was as dispassionate as his attitude had been back yonder when they'd left the wounded renegade. Jawn was also dispassionate. He had the money pouch.

Ben said, 'Her kind don't get lost. My guess is that she went back to the gut-shot renegade . . . they're clanny even when they are enemies. Don't worry, she's taken a shine to you. You couldn't lose the old witch if you wanted to.'

They rested three times before the pre-dawn chill indicated the near-advent of a new day. After the last halt Ben changed direction slightly. By poor pre-dawn light Killian could see that they were heading north-easterly. He could make out that they were heading into steeper and more heavily timbered country not far from the nearly abrupt rise of the land toward the peaks which marked the spine of the mountains they had been riding through since the day before.

Their final halt was in a burned-over clearing of about a hundred acres. The fire which had devastated this area had to have burned through some years earlier because the grass was stirrup high. There was a piddling little cold-water creek.

It happened to be the only grassy place for miles. They discovered that it was the property of wild animals, not because it was grassy, but because grazing animals came here for the grass, and were followed by other animals, the kind that lived off the meat of the grass eaters.

All Killian knew of the time was that it was colder

than it had been which signified the nearness of dawn. As he squatted between Jawn and Ben, who produced three sticks of jerky and gave one to George, one to Jawn, the Arkansan said, 'Another three, four miles. It used to be a buffler hunters' camp. At one time there was about six or eight log houses up there. Last time I passed through the houses was fallin' down . . . I knew an old hide-hunter named Jasper. Spent a few days with him once years back . . . In'ians got him. He could talk good but he was deef as a post.'

The hobbled horses cropped grass like it was going out of season, and while grass was the mainstay of horses during summer, they could not gain a pound of weight on grass alone with the kind of use these horses had been getting. They needed grain. Where the three men hunkered with saddle blankets around their shoulders, any kind of grain but especially rolled barley was as unheard of as life among the stars.

Ben had pondered while riding. Now, he put his thoughts into words. 'Them bastards must've ranged over considerable territory to know where Big Timber was. I'd guess it's been close to thirty years since anyone's lived up there.'

Killian broke into the other man's reminiscences when he heard something across the clearing, among the charred old punky stumps over there.

Ben briefly cocked his head before saying, 'Bear.' As Jawn walked out to the horses Ben said, 'Bears kill a lot of horses. Folks think of bears as big, clumsy critters. Mister Killian, I'm here to tell you I've seen a bear run alongside a horse and keep it up until the horse changed course. That's how he got away. Bears is fast but they're heavy and pigeon-toed an' not real handy at changin' course the way horses do.'

Their animals were no longer grazing. They were standing motionless, heads up, little ears pointing in the direction of a large animal brushing small trees aside, trampling brush and making growling sounds as it approached. Jawn stood among them.

Ben had a cud in his cheek, he sank to one knee leaning on his Winchester, slowly masticating. All Killian knew of bears was that they were troublesome and fearless. Ambrose had told him of a fight he'd had with a she-bear who had a pair of cubs. Ambrose had said if an old sow-bear has young with her, get out of her way as fast as you can.

Killian also knelt, leaned on his saddle gun and listened to the animal neither of them could see.

Ben casually said, 'Big one, Mister Killian. Most likely a boar bear. We dassn't shoot, they'll hear the noise for miles an' this close to Big Timber. . . . There it is. It's a big one for a fact. Big old boar bear.' George agreed. 'It's a big one.'

The animal came into view, visible in the poor light only because it was moving. It broke clear of the last cover, paused to stand on its hind legs with its nose tilted and swinging from side to side.

Ben said, 'When he's closer we got to run at him yellin'.'

Killian watched the bear, guessed it weighed close to

a ton and said, 'What if we don't scare him?'

Ben's reply was short. 'Rip off dry bark from some of the stumps an' fire 'em. About the only thing a bear'll run from is fire.'

Killian looked around. There were rotting stumps in the burned-over clearing but none were close. He turned back to watching the bear.

Ben said, 'He's scented up the horses.'

The bear seemed to be in no hurry. Twice he stopped to rear up and test for scent. Killian had seen many bears but this one was larger standing up than any other bear he had seen.

Their hobbled horses were rigid with fear. They could not flee and the fastest hopping hobbled horse on earth could not outrace a bear. Jawn soothed them with quiet words.

One of the horses began hopping westward. The bear reared up, watched briefly, dropped down and came ahead a little faster. Ben said, Now!' and jumped waving his Winchester and yelling at the top of his voice. George and the 'breed did the same.

The bear was startled enough to stop stone still. Killian did not believe the bear would retreat. Bears had reason to fear men but not all bears understood how deadly the two-legged things were. This bear finally sat back on his haunches watching the men yelling and running at him. Visibility was not good enough for the men to see the bear move—or not move.

They were less than sixty feet from the old boar, who still sat on his haunches watching them, when Killian stumbled over a dead limb no longer than his arm and as thick through. Ben paused only long enough to see George regain his balance and come up holding the limb that had tripped him. George ran until he was able to overtake the Arkansan then halted and threw the stick as hard as he could. It hit the bear a glancing blow on the side of the head. All bears are brave, some are even heroic but this one wasn't, he let go a bellow of pain, swung around and ran. Ben stopped, watched the bear then faced George. 'That was good aim. It hit the old boar near the eye where it's tender.'

Killian said nothing. He would not have wagered a plugged penny the bear would not have charged before the piece of wood hit him and the fact that it had hit him was pure accident.

Ben leaned on his Winchester sucking air and listening to the sounds of the retreating animal before wagging his head, hoisting the gun to his shoulder and turning back. As the three of them passed the terrified horses Jawn used his softest voice to reassure them. He might as well have said nothing at all. It would be at least an hour before the smell of the bear would fade.

They rigged out with the first silvery strands showing in the east. Even after the sun was climbing it would remain gloomy among the trees.

Ben held the lead for about an hour before halting, tying his horse by the reins to a scantling fir and waiting until George and Jawn had done the same before moving ahead on foot.

Dawn was near and the chill at this elevation came

close to being frost. Ben moved like a panther using every scrap of cover as he advanced. Killian followed the lanky man's example. They finally halted on timbered high slope where Ben leaned on a tree looking down into a good-sized clearing. In the distance they could make out log houses whose degree of dilapidation would not be discernible until the light improved.

Ben said, 'Elk feed in a place like this . . . you see any?'

Killian shook his head without speaking. The Big Timber settlement was both picturesque and spectacular; it had high peaks to the north and less impressive lower upthrusts to the east and west.

Ben said, 'Where are the horses? They should be grazin' down there.' He spat amber. 'You don't expect we rode all the way up here for nothin', do you?'

As before Killian remained silent. He thought he had caught a glimpse of movement on the westerly curve of the big clearing.

Ben suddenly said, 'That beats all. Watch yonder to the west. You see 'em?'

George nodded. 'I see one. There should be two.'

Ben stiffly watched as a solitary rider came into the clearing. Not until a second rider appeared did he speak, then all he said was, 'Hell; they should've been up here already.'

The riders crossed to the least dilapidated house, tied up out front, disappeared inside briefly, then returned to lead their animals out a-ways, hobble them and haul their riding equipment back to the log house.

Ben smiled. 'Give 'em time to settle in before we sneak down there an' set them horses loose.'

They sat on the ridge, watched pale smoke rise from a mud-wattle chimney, and although the sun had cleared the easterly horizon, it had not yet reached into the Big Timber clearing.

Jawn wrinkled his nose. 'I hope they don't eat it all. I'm hungry enough to eat a skunk beginnin' at the rear if someone would hold its head.' Ben arose, dusted his britches and jerked his head for the others to follow. He had assessed the area, knew what they should do and moved on as he usually did, like a wraith.

In Killian's view the problem was not leaving the lookout, it wasn't even getting to the last tiers of trees around the meadow. The problem was how to move out where there was no cover but grass to reach the renegade's horses.

Ben stopped where they could stand protected from discovery, took his time slicing off a fresh cud and cheeked it. He glanced once at his companions and began following the forest's fringe around in a southerly direction. His strategy was clear to Killian, Ben meant to either go completely around the clearing or to its southernmost border before trying to reach the hobbled horses, who had not cooperated at all. If they had grazed along as horses commonly do, they might in time have come to the lower end of the meadow, but they hadn't moved more than a few yards from the centre of the clearing since being put out there, which simply meant that they had come a considerable distance without feed, and were hungry enough not to lift their heads nor move more than a few yards as they grazed.

Jawn suddenly threw up an arm to keep George motionless. Two more riders entered the clearing, but these men came from the north, the direction of those formidable back-grounding peaks.

8

One Dead One to Go

Ben stood a long time beside a forest monarch. He and Jawn were as dumbfounded as Killian was at the arrival of two more riders. Ben eventually said, 'Ain't supposed to be but two of 'em an In'ian, an' a white.'

Killian gazed up the clearing where a stringy tendril of grey smoke was rising. He had no explanation for the arrival of two more men but he made a guess. 'Maybe it's more of the renegades. Maybe they've used this place to rendezvous before.'

Ben nodded. 'Likely . . . well, that makes things different.' He faced Killian to speak when Jawn said, 'Look.' A man had emerged from the cabin. He stood a moment gazing southward then hiked out where the horses were and Ben said, 'You get a good look at him, did you?'

George's reply was curt. 'Pickett!'

Ben nodded. 'An' that answers the question about

who the others are don't it? When they scattered Pickett an' another one headed up here. I'd guess they had longer to ride or they'd have got here sooner.'

They retreated deeper into the timber, eventually went back to care for their animals and while they were doing this Ben said, 'When the odds was better we could take chances. Now, figurin' calls for somethin' different. Ain't any way for us to get at them horses in broad daylight, tall grass or not, an' if it comes to a fight I'll tell you grass don't stop bullets. We got to wait for evenin'.'

There were two bothersome aspects of waiting. One, the most important, was that feed had to be found for the horses. The second concern was food for themselves. They had no more jerky and only God knew where Catlin and her parfleche bag were.

The answer to the first problem was simple; they took the horses back to the first small clearing, hobbled them and watched the animals do as the renegades' horses had done, drop their heads to crop grass without moving. Since there was nothing to be attempted until dusk, they talked and loafed, until Ben's taciturnity eventually returned. It was directly associated with his shrunken gut.

Eventually they returned to the rise where they could see the cabin. There no longer was smoke rising and two men, both Indians were outside in plain sight. Killian thought they had to feel safe. Ben thought so too and said, 'They're careless. That'll favor us come dark but right now I'm hungry.'

Killian made a suggestion, 'Sooner or later someone's going to go out into the bushes. If we could catch one.'

Ben's disgusted look silenced the younger man. Ben said, 'If one comes up missin'. . . . An' we don't want a prisoner, we want jerky, or somethin' better.'

Killian said no more.

Later, two of the renegades brought in their animals to be rigged out. They called back and forth as they were doing this but the distance was too great, none of the men on the ridge could hear what was being said.

Those two men left the clearing riding northerly in the direction from which they had come.

Time passed, Ben withdrew deeper into the forest gloom and slept. Killian should also have been that tired but something in the clearing held his attention. A man came out of the cabin carrying a bedroll with a pair of saddle-bags over his shoulder. He left these things outside, went out to the horses and brought one back with him. It was a big, ugly sorrel with the kind of build only strong animals had. George watched as the animal was rigged out, went back to shake Ben awake. They both watched the renegade mount up riding due west. Ben got up, grunted something and hurried to the place where they had hobbled their animals. Jawn and Killian followed.

Ben led off on a roundabout way to reach the forested country westerly making no attempt to pick up the sign of the man who had left the cabin. They made good time. George thought the Arkansan was seeking to get in front of the rider they were pursuing.

In their favor was the fact that the renegade did not know he was being hunted. When Ben was satisfied they were far enough ahead he turned northward, dismounted with his head cocked, listening, then signalled to Jawn and George to also dismount. They made no attempt to hide their horses, instead they sifted through forest gloom in the direction of the oncoming rider until they could clearly hear him, then stepped behind trees with enough distance between them to be on both sides of the renegade when he appeared.

The sounds of fir needles being crushed under shod hooves became louder but they were never more than a whisper. At no place in the timber except for the occasional clearing was there hard ground.

The man came into sight several minutes before he was to be waylaid. It was a white man, unshaven, soiled-looking, with close-spaced eyes and a lantern jaw. He had a saddle-gun under his right leg and on the same side he wore a six-gun in a scarred holster.

Killian watched the Arkansan. When Ben raised his Winchester taking a brace against a tree, George did the same. The renegade rode right down their gunsights. When Ben spoke the man jerked out of a slouch. Ben said, 'Hold it right there, mister!'

The big sorrel horse planted his forelegs firmly, ears pointing. Ben said, 'Get down. Mister, be careful, I ain't alone. You even look like you're goin' to get nasty an' you'll get yourself killed. Get down!'

The man swung to the ground, moved to the head of

his horse and saw Ben where he stepped clear of his tree. Ben lowered the Winchester, held it across his lower body in both hands and cocked.

The renegade had eyes like a weasel. He had a bloodless slit of a mouth, a wiry build with a mop of unshorn brown hair. He also had the beginning of a beard with a reddish tint.

Ben said, 'Shuck the sidearm,' and after the renegade had disarmed himself Ben said, 'Jawn, empty his pockets.'

The 'breed went forward, systematically robbed the snake-eyed individual, found not one pouch but two, which he held aloft for Ben to see as he said, 'We're gettin' closer.' Jawn shoved the pouches inside his shirt, turned up a belly-gun and a boot knife, both of which he appropriated.

Ben asked where the man was going and got a sullen reply. 'Out of these hills.'

'Where, out of these hills . . . Jawn, stick the knife under his chin . . . where out of these hills, mister?'

With his own knife forcing his head back the man said, 'No particular place, just away from here.'

'Where's them others goin' who rode north?'

'Over the rim an' down the other side to a place called Beaverton. They got homes there an' women.'

Ben relaxed without easing the dog down on his Winchester. 'Who's left in the cabin back yonder?'

The renegade's close-set eyes showed defiance as he replied, 'Go back there and find out.'

Jawn drew blood, moved the blade to the side of the

renegade's neck and looked over his shoulder. Ben told the outlaw he was as close to hell as he would ever be, then repeated the question. 'Who's left back yonder?'

This time the sullen voice answered quickly. 'Hendry Pickett an' Long Tree.'

'Long Tree an In'ian?'

'Yes, an' a real mean one.'

'Is that a fact? Do you fellers use the old Big Timber camp to meet?'

'Yes . . . and I'll tell you somethin' else, mister. Them two that left earlier ridin' north is comin' back—with a herd of holdout In'ians. You take my advice, get on your horses an' don't even look back.'

Ben spat, ran a sleeve across his lips and eyed the renegade. 'What's your name?'

'John Smith.'

'John Smith, why did you shoot that squatter woman down yonder?'

'I didn't shoot her, Hendry did when she was slow makin' up a food bundle. We was in a hurry.'

Killian removed the saddle-bags and took them aside to open them. Jawn watched this but Ben did not take his eyes off the snake-eyed renegade. He softly said, 'I got reason for killin' renegades any place I find 'em. . . . This is far as you go, John Smith.'

The renegade's reply was true. 'You pull that trigger, an' they'll hear you back at the camp, an' maybe where them other two is bringin' back the holdouts.'

Ben eased down the hammer of his Winchester, leaned it against a tree and walked toward John Smith, whose tongue made a quick circuit of his lips and whose shifty eyes fled and returned before he spoke again. 'You got my money, you can take my gatherings off the animal. Just leave me the horse. I quit Pickett. I had enough.'

Ben stopped, held out his hand and Jawn placed the knife in it. What followed horrified George Killian. Ben stabbed John Smith to the hilt, watched the man crumple, spat and handed the knife back to Jawn.

The 'breed's reaction matched his partner's mood. He did not look down he simply said, 'What about the horse and his gatherings?'

'Dump his bedroll and whatnot an' turn the horse loose. Head it on westerly so's it don't figure to go back to them other horses.' Ben turned toward Killian. 'Let's see about settlin' with Pickett before them others return—if they return.' He looked at the dead man before also saying, 'Son of bitches like that one'd lie on their mother's grave. All the same, let's go back.'

By the time they had retraced their tracks Killian still had difficulty finding justification for that murder. When they returned to the ridge overlooking the Big Timber clearing Killian was beginning to think he did not belong in this raw, brutal world.

Ben stood beside his horse for a long time watching the cabin and the hobbled horses in the meadow before turning to say, 'Maybe there ain't no In'ian. Let's get this over with.'

He led them around the curve of their ridge until they were not only above the cabin but behind it. Like most cabins this one had no rear window. Jawn mumbled something which was indistinguishable to Killian but which Ben understood because he said, 'Yes. Like other times.' Then he faced Killian. 'You go down to the south end of the clearing an' ride up. The horse will most likely nicker . . . Pickett'll come out to see why. He'll see you an' we'll kill the son of a bitch from behind.'

It was not a suggestion, it was an order. Ben expected no discussion. Jawn looked at Killian, nodded and got back astride. They left George standing beside his animal.

Eventually he mounted and rode back around the way they had recently come. He had never developed the widespread custom among frontiersmen of talking to his horse, but this time he did.

He told the horse Ben was a murderer pure and simple, that why he murdered was beside the point, which simply was that he killed people any way he could.

When he got to the south end of the clearing he reined northward, came out of the trees and walked his horse in the direction of the hobbled animal, which was about mid-way along.

The horse saw a mounted man coming toward him, raised its head to watch, and did not move until Killian was within a few hundred feet, then it hopped out of Killian's path. It did not whinny, it snorted. It also hopped farther away, stopped, threw up its head and loudly snorted again.

Killian watched the cabin not the horse. No one appeared. He rode on a loose rein. There was no sign of Ben or Jawn nor did he expect there to be. If there ever were two individuals who could move through big timber shadows like spirits it was those two.

Still no one appeared from the cabin. Killian's mouth was dry. Being a clay pigeon was nothing Killian nor anyone else relished, and the closer he got to the doorway without anyone appearing the more he sweated.

Finally the hobbled horse, well west and to the rear of Killian whinnied.

The man who appeared outside the door was looking northward, evidently expecting to see riders coming from that direction. He did not look southward until Killian was no more than ten yards distant when his reaction was to pull straight up. He was not wearing his belt-gun. He finally came un-tracked, stepped back, reached around the door casing and straightened forward with a Winchester in both hands.

When Killian was closer the large, bearded man looked across the clearing and on both sides of it. To George it seemed he did not believe an outsider would ride straight up the meadow in plain sight. The bearded man was right, Killian was not alone.

The big man called to Killian to stop, which George did. Any moment now Ben and Jawn would cut the large man down.

'Who the hell are you an' what're you doin' up here?' the large man called.

George watched for his companions, did not see either of them and groped for an answer to the big man. He finally shouted back, 'Passing through.'

The large man called again. 'Ride closer.' He also shifted the Winchester so that it was aimed.

George eased ahead at a slow walk. He should've had his six-gun in his lap. It was too late now to remedy that oversight.

The large man's brow slowly creased. 'You're the feller from them cabins back yonder a few days ago. What's your name?'

Killian got no chance to reply. From the northwest corner of the cabin Ben stepped into view with a fisted six-gun. 'His name's Killian, you murderin' son of a bitch!'

The large man reacted almost before Ben had stopped speaking. He snapped off a wild shot and threw himself backwards.

Ben was ready. He fired; echoes carried in all directions. A long splinter of punky wood flew from the door frame. Jawn appeared around the opposite corner of the cabin. He saw the shattered wood and stared. At that range he had never known Ben to miss.

Ben yelled for Killian to go up the slope eastward which George did without hesitation. From a slit in the south side of the cabin the cornered renegade tried a shot but Killian's horse was moving too fast.

Silence settled but not for long. Ben shouted to the bearded man. 'This shack'll burn like pine sap. You come out or burn up!'

There was no answer.

Ben hugged the log wall, gestured for Jawn to go around back. They had already agreed about Jawn setting the fire.

Up the hill Killian stood beside his wind-sucking horse. The man inside the cabin was going to die one way or another, he was satisfied about that. He tied the horse, took his saddle gun and began descending the hill behind the cabin where Jawn saw him and ignored Killian as he furiously whittled dry kindling.

Ben eased along the front of the cabin. There was one window. In former times it had been covered by scraped-thin rawhide which allowed heat and light to penetrate but which could not be seen through. Now, only fragments of that window covering still hung around the opening.

Ben stopped flat on the north side of the window, listened, heard nothing and raised his handgun. He could have called upon the large man to pitch his weapons out and follow them with both arms over his head, but he didn't. He did not want the large man alive.

He threw a wild shot through the window opening. Before the echo died the man inside fired back. Neither of them hit anything and had not expected to.

When Killian reached the rear wall Jawn was swearing. He could not get the wood to burn, it was too old and punky, it would smolder but even with both Jawn and Killian blowing on it all they got was clouds of smoke.

Jawn ran up the slope to the nearest big tree, used his

knife to pry loose bark and returned panting. This time he got fire, but only on the outside of the bark, the inside was too green to burn. When he held the puny flames to the cabin's wall there was more smoke but the logs too were punky.

Jawn looked at Killian. 'It ain't goin' to work.' He looked up the hill and said, 'Come along.'

They went back up the hill to a huge old mossy boulder, Jawn sighted first then he and Killian put all their strength into moving the boulder. Probably a span of mules could have dislodged it from its eons-old bed but two men couldn't.

Jawn had another idea. They got down on hands and knees in front of the rock and gouged needles and soil like a pair of gophers.

It took a lot of digging but eventually, when they got behind the massive boulder they could move it a little. They took a breather before trying again. This time Killian found a heavy limb which they jockeyed beneath the boulder, strained hard, and finally the huge rock tipped into the hand-dug trough and its own weight did the rest.

It gathered momentum as it went down the slope. Killian and Jawn stood transfixed watching and waiting. When the boulder struck a small, flatter boulder behind the cabin a short distance it was catapulted into the air. When it smashed into the rear wall of the cabin the sound was loud as rotten old logs yielded to the massive rock. It crashed through the wall, stopped half in, half out, other logs quivered, the smell of ancient dust and punky wood rose overhead. Inside, someone let out a squawk.

Jawn grinned through sweat from ear to ear and started down the slope. Around front Ben was startled by the explosive sound of the boulder breaking through the rear wall. He had no idea what had happened except that whatever it was, it had shaken the old cabin on its fir foundation and the man inside had yelped.

He threw another shot through the window. This time there was no answering shot. He paused to plug in two fresh loads and pitched a stone inside. He did not expect this to produce a hostile reaction and he was right, it didn't.

He leaned close and called. 'You smell smoke?'

There was no reply. Ben tried again, beginning to wonder if that boulder hadn't caught the man inside. 'You're not goin' nowhere. Folks'll find your bones in the ash.'

Again there was silence.

Ben was tempted to risk a quick peek through the window but prudence held him back. The smell of smoke was strong. He had no way of knowing there was no fire around back. Neither did the cornered renegade.

Finally the renegade shouted, 'There's help on the way, you miserable bastards. All I got to do is wait you out. They'll skin you and make jerky from the meat.'

Jawn and Killian appeared around the southwest corner of the cabin. Ben hand-signed for Jawn to creep along the front wall until he was on the far side of the window. Killian remained back as Jawn began sidling. When he was close Ben nodded. They both leaned as far as they dared and fired four times, raking the cabin's interior from side to side, and this time they heard something, a man swearing through gritted teeth.

Jawn would have peeked in but Ben growled and shook his head. The smoke was dissipating, the man inside was silent, Killian was squinting northward where he had thought he had detected shadowy forms in the forest gloom.

Ben looked at Jawn, reset his hat and sprang around where he could see inside. A carbine shot carried his hat away like a bird. He jumped back as Jawn removed his hat, crouched low below the window and sprang upright. He had seconds to look inside before dropping down. This time there was no gunshot from the cornered renegade.

Jawn used hand gestures to indicate that Pickett was sitting upright along the north wall. Jawn made the sign for a gunshot and pressed the bullet-fist against his own body in the lower body.

Ben called one last time. 'We're comin' in.'

This time there was a reply, in a rough voice that lacked vigor or force. 'Come ahead, I like company.' This was followed by the sound of the renegade levering a bullet into the chamber of his Winchester.

Jawn looked where Killian was gesturing in the direction of the distant hobbled horse. When Jawn simply frowned Killian spoke without raising his voice. 'There's no In'ian in there with him—there's only one horse.'

9

Real Trouble

Ben ducked under the window, came upright outside the door, kicked it and jumped back. The gunshot inside the cabin sounded unusually loud. Ben heard the gun being levered, spun to the window, saw the man inside and fired twice as fast as he could pull the trigger. He jumped to his right, heard the gun clatter to the floor, waited for the man inside to either retrieve the Winchester or cock his belt-gun, and when he heard neither sound he moved cat-like back to the window, took down a breath and stepped ahead until he was framed in the window from the chest up.

The man was sitting against the north wall. There was blood showing and his head was slumped forward.

Ben kept the cocked six-gun in his right hand, leaned as far as he could, raised the inside door-bar, pulled back and entered the cabin.

Jawn came along cautiously, cocked pistol raised. Even when Ben spoke the 'breed hesitated before entering. Ben said, 'The son of a bitch ain't dead.'

Killian appeared later, after the Arkansan and his partner had emptied the wounded man's pockets. What

George saw from the doorway was a sight he would never forget. His two companions callously rolled the large bearded man to empty his pockets. They also flung him on his back, ripped the blood-soaked shirt, unbuckled the money belt and yanked it out. It too was soaked with blood.

Hendry Pickett was not dead. He was as limp as a wet rag and occasionally groaned but until they flung him on his back Killian did not see his eyes, wide open, and his bearded lips which also moved when he said, 'I'll take . . . you to hell . . . with me.'

Jawn straightened up a little. He had felt that no one who had lost so much blood could still be alive, but Ben wiped his hands on an old blue bandanna, shook his head slightly and replied in his normal tone of voice, 'You ain't goin' to kill nobody. That squatter woman you shot—remember her?' As Ben finished speaking he held out his hand toward Jawn, who pulled out the knife he had taken from the snake-eyed man they had caught west of the clearing, put it in Ben's hand and rocked back on his heels to watch.

Killian spoke from the doorway. 'Let him die in peace.' He moved across the devastated room, caught Ben's wrist in a powerful grip and twisted until the knife fell. He kicked the knife away.

Jawn's eyes were round in disbelief. Ben looked up at Killian while massaging one wrist with the fingers of his other hand. He did not say a word.

Killian glanced at Hendry Pickett, looked away then back again. Pickett was looking straight up from sightless eyes. Killian picked up the knife and dropped it beside Ben. 'Go ahead. Use it. He's dead.'

The two men on their knees leaned, saw the drying eyes and rocked back to rise. Ben looked around the cabin, saw the huge boulder three-quarters of the way through the rear wall, spat and went to the doorway to look out and around.

A gunshot echoed among the northerly timber. The slug missed by yards, ploughed up soil several feet from the cabin southerly, and muffled echoes lingered even after Ben had jumped back inside.

Jawn did a foolish thing. He went to the window to lean and look northward. It may have been shadows which saved him or it could have been the wild, keening scream from that direction, but whatever it was it made Jawn pull swiftly back as he yelled at Ben. 'In'ians!'

Even Killian's attention was distracted. He picked up Pickett's revolver, checked it for loads, found it had been shot out and dropped it as Ben slammed the door and barred it.

For the first time since their original meeting Killian saw something close to fear on the face of the Arkansan, but when Ben spoke his voice was normal. He said, 'They come back with some hideouts,' and sounded mildly surprised.

A white man shouted from the northward forest. 'Hendry? . . . Hendry, who's in there with you?'

Killian shook his head. Why had they fired at Ben if they hadn't been sure it wasn't a friend with Pickett?

Possibly what had happened since the death of Ambrose and the destruction of his cabins may have followed some form of logic—maybe the frontier variety—but some of it made no sense at all to George Killian—except their present predicament, holed up in a dilapidated log cabin, and that didn't make much sense either.

If Ben and Jawn hadn't wasted time robbing Hendry Pickett they all could have been a-horseback by now and away from the clearing.

He stopped conjecturing as another of those wild screams echoed out across the clearing where the horse raised its head. It might have heard a war-whoop before, and it might only have reacted to the unmistakable fury of that noise.

Ben calmly retrieved Pickett's weapons, yanked loads from the dead man's bloody shell belt, reloaded each weapon and as he passed Killian he said, 'Well now— how many is there?'

Silence settled after the man who had called before shouted again.

'Hendry? You all right? Who's in there with you. This is Wallis. Me'n Frank brought back some help.'

Ben tried a ruse. 'How many, Wallis?'

There was no answer. In fact that ended the talk. Killian shook his head. Even accepting that drawling way Ben spoke, his voice had a nasal twang to it which it was doubtful that Hendry Pickett had possessed. In fact, Ben's voice was unique in just about any place on earth except Arkansas.

Time passed, Ben paced the cabin from front to back. Where that boulder had smashed the rear wall, there were places men would be able to see inside. He stationed Jawn back there. He chewed, spat and listened. Killian only listened.

There was not a sound, even the raucous blue jays who inhabited the uplands were gone. Killian flung an old soiled canvas ground cloth over Hendry Pickett.

A coyote yapped and was answered from the westerly, forested side of the clearing. Ben spat. 'Surround. Depends on how many. What we got to worry about is the busted back wall. They'll try sneakin' along that slope directly and come down behind the house.'

A recognizable sound followed the Arkansan's words. They all knew what it meant. Their besiegers had not only slipped out where the hobbled horse was and had freed it, they had also found three other horses and had stampeded them southward too.

Ben made a harsh grunt of a laugh. 'Jawn, you figure we'll get that saloon?'

The 'breed did not take his eyes off what he could see of the rearward slope when he answered, 'We'll get it.'

Ben grunted again. Killian got the impression that the Arkansan believed they would all die in the cabin.

He thought that too, but like the others, on the rare occasions when George spoke, nothing like that was mentioned.

One thing bothered Killian. 'Daylight doesn't last for ever. What are they waiting for?'

Ben replied dryly. 'More'n likely that's what they're

waitin' for the same as we done.' Ben aimed and spat out the window.

Those two coyotes exchanged yelps again, but this time the one across the clearing was farther south and the other one was getting close to the rear of the cabin along that rim up there.

Jawn stealthily eased his carbine in an opening between the boulder and the broken wall. Ben and Killian watched. Jawn very cautiously lowered his head and snugged back the butt plate. Killian held his breath. Ben's jaws stopped moving. Moments passed. Jawn finally said, 'Son of a bitch! Maybe light bounced off my barrel. That tomahawk run like a rabbit an' got behind a tree.'

Ben resumed masticating. George resumed breathing. Jawn removed his carbine from the aiming place, leaned it aside and leaned forward to peek up the slope. The bullet and the sound of the up-hill gunshot seemed to arrive simultaneously. The echo wore itself out over distance but the bullet struck Jawn's side of the boulder and flattened there. If Jawn had not leaned back to put his weapon aside it probably would have hit him.

Ben made another dry remark. 'That wasn't no In'ian, that was a real sharpshooter.'

It was warmer outside than it was inside but was warm enough for the besieged to drink from several canteens and Jawn found a sack of elk jerky which he passed around. He also found several tins of fruit and a round loaf of bread that could have been rolled half-way to Bridgerville before it cracked. But it went down with the aid of water.

While they were eating the Arkansan said, 'My guess is that there ain't many of 'em, maybe no more'n five or six. If there was a herd of 'em they would have surrounded the meadow an' closed in by now.'

Killian looked at the lanky man. 'Five or six.'

'It's a guess, Mister Killian. Maybe a few more.'

Killian was turning toward the window when he also said, 'Five or six, ten or twenty, if we don't get out of this cabin it's not going to matter how many there are. They can sluice-shot in here the way we did. The difference is there'll be more bullets comin' in this time.'

Ben worried off a piece of jerky, said nothing until he had worked it to manageable size, then he addressed Killian. 'I'm favorable to the notion of gettin' out of here—just how do we do it, Mister Killian?'

'The same way they expect to get in here. In the night?'

Ben ruminated. 'T'won't be easy, Mister Killian. They'll have crawled as close as they can. Open that door, Mister Killian, an' they'll make a sieve out of you.'

George turned on the lanky man. 'It's that or get slaughtered in here isn't it?'

Jawn looked at his partner, Ben considered the canvas-covered corpse and nodded.

They finished most of the jerky, emptied one of the canteens—and waited.

Jawn returned to his rear wall but more carefully this

time. He eased his head down an inch or two at a time until he could see behind the cabin. He did not get into position to look up the slope, the last time he tried that he came within an ace of getting his head blown off.

Ben eventually said, 'Ain't much point in bein' in this country if a man's afoot.'

Neither Jawn nor Killian responded. Killian was standing back several feet from the window looking out. Interior shadows protected him but visibility was limited to the area directly westward and it was closed off on both sides.

If there were men across the clearing in the timber they were hidden by the everlasting gloom. He was turning away when swift movement caught his attention. An Indian wearing a filthy whiteman shirt of bright red flickered briefly as he moved from one tree to a more distant tree.

Killian said nothing but continued to watch, ready to believe other Indians would also be passing southward, but no other Indians appeared. He sighed and went to sit on one of the three rickety home-made chairs in the room. It really was not going to matter how many Indians were out there; bottled up in the old cabin was not unlike being caught in a trap.

Jawn abruptly broke the silence, he was back kneeling beside the corpse from which he had flung the canvas aside.

He arose holding something limp and bloody in one hand. He went over to Ben as he said, 'Look at this.'

Ben went to the table to spread the piece of wet

paper flat. He bent over it a long time before speaking while still leaning on the table. 'Where did you find it, Jawn?'

'There was a little pocket sewed into the back of his shirt. What is it?'

Ben did not answer the question immediately, he looked in the direction of the north wall where Pickett had been leaning. 'So that's what the son of a bitch was tryin' to do against that wall.'

Ben crossed to the patch of blood where Pickett had propped himself after being wounded the first time, stood a moment studying the wall, then yanked aside an old deer hide and said, 'I'll be damned. A cache.'

Prying the logs apart was not difficult. He used Pickett's own knife to do it. Where the log had been sawed and refitted was a shallow cache. Inside it were two bundles of greenbacks tied with a leather thong and four sticks of dynamite along with a tightly wound coil of oily fuse.

'Now just what'n hell did he figure to use this stuff for?' Ben asked aloud.

Killian risked a guess. 'Blow open a safe? Blow up a railroad bridge?'

Ben replied while pocketing the rolls of greenbacks before removing the wax-paper-wrapped dynamite sticks. 'You're likely right.'

He moved to the table, placed the dynamite atop it and stood silently considering his find for a long time. It was Jawn who broke his silence.

'What can we do with it, Ben?'

'Maybe use it to get out of here.'

'How, Ben?'

'Shut up, Jawn.'

Killian returned to peering out the window. He saw nothing but slanting shadows. The day was wearing along, which did nothing to reassure him. As he turned the lanky man said, 'If we could get 'em all to palaver—'

Jawn broke in. 'An' pitch one of them sticks into the midst of 'em!'

Ben looked displeased about being interrupted but nodded his head. Jawn then annoyed him further by saying, 'How? Them bastards got no reason to want to palaver.'

Although Ben was annoyed, this time he simply shook his head. What Jawn said was true. On top of that, those renegades would never approach the cabin in plain sight while the men inside were alive.

Killian had a suggestion. 'If one of us could sneak out of here, go north into the trees, find their horses.'

'Mister Killian,' Ben interrupted to say, 'do you believe in Santa Claus? Them ain't squatters or emigrants out there. Them is men who been readin' sign since babyhood!'

'In the dark?' Killian exclaimed. 'One of us? While they're concentrating on the cabin, closing in on it? Ben; sitting in here like caged rats. We're going to get killed! Anything is better than waiting for that isn't it? And yes, I believe in Santa Claus! We have to believe in something, we don't have anything else left.'

Not another word was spoken for a long time. Killian went to the table, picked up one of the sticks of dynamite and spoke again. 'This isn't going to help us. Even if we had a box of it.' He put the stick down and paced forward with his back to the frontiersmen.

Jawn looked at Ben, who was regarding Killian's back. One of those coyotes sounded again, from around the lower end of the clearing and part way up the east side. His answer came from the north, somewhere between the timber line and the cabin.

Killian faced around. 'Does that mean they're getting closer?'

Ben nodded without speaking.

Jawn spoke and his words surprised Killian, who had formed an opinion that the 'breed had no great reasoning ability. Jawn said, 'Shoot inside the cabin. Make it sound like we got into a fight in here. Then set an' wait for 'em to get curious enough to come see.'

Ben frowned at the 'breed before turning to Killian as though seeking an opinion. Killian told them essentially what he had before. 'Anything is better than waiting for them to storm the cabin. It might work. What the hell, we have plenty of ammunition.'

As he finished speaking Killian fired into the sod and the log ceiling. Dust flew. Jawn shot into the north wall twice and yelled curses at the top of his voice. The last of them to use his handgun was the Arkansan. He too fired into the north wall and loudly cursed.

Gunsmoke was thick by the time they stopped firing. It was not an altogether unpleasant scent but neither was it anything people would ordinarily go out of their way to smell.

When silence returned it was deathless, both inside the cabin and beyond it. They waited hoping hard, and not convinced the ruse would work. It was the waiting that was hardest. The sun continued its westerly slide when Ben finally shook his head. Before he could speak, if he had intended to, a flurry of wild gunfire sent bullets through the window. The men inside pressed flat against the south wall until firing ended. Ben blew out a ragged breath before saying, 'That was close.'

Killian ignored the gunfire. 'They wanted to know if someone would fire back. Let them sweat.'

Whether the attackers sweated or not, unlikely as the heat diminished, they had a high degree of anxiety. They would not have to run a risk by storming the cabin after dark if there were only dead men inside.

Ben cheeked a fresh cud. Jawn reminded him his plug was getting very small. Killian went over to stand back in shadows looking out the window. The land was still and silent without motion of any kind. He went back to the south wall where Ben and the 'breed were leaning. Jawn said, 'See anything?'

Killian shook his head.

One of those coyotes sounded. This time it was up the slope behind the cabin.

Jawn returned to his shattered back wall and leaned to peek out. There was nothing for him to see unless he exposed himself as he had done before in order to see to the top of the slope, which he did not do. One near thing was enough.

Something bumped the north wall. The three defenders fastened their eyes in that direction. The sound was not repeated. Ben said, 'White man. Clumsy bastard.'

Whoever had got up this close could go in one of two directions, around front to peek in the window, or around back to peek through one of the shattered places. Killian arose, got into position against the front wall with his back to the door. He could see anyone approaching from the north.

Ben went over to the back wall, leaned and listened. Jawn stood near the old table unwilling to peek out beside the rock again, not with one—maybe more than one—skulker very close to the cabin.

10

The Unexpected

It seemed as though the entire world was holding its breath. There was no sound of any kind. The "coyotes" were up the rear slope, someone had been along the north wall and was probably along the back wall now.

The sun continued its inexorable slide toward a saw-toothed rim of jagged peaks. The wait was hard on the men inside whose nerves had already been scraped raw. The lanky Arkansan was no longer chewing.

Killian's back was to the door as he watched the rear wall. The bloody scrap of paper along with four sticks of dynamite were on the rickety table. Hendry Pickett was bloating under the canvas. The interior of the cabin was a ruin with bloodstains almost everywhere men looked.

Outside behind the cabin someone made a keening, whistling sound. Ben glanced toward the rear wall and braced himself.

Jawn couldn't have raised a smile if his life had depended on it and George Killian seemed to be scarcely breathing. Clearly, that whistle had been a signal of some kind, most likely to start the final attack.

Jawn saw a shadowy phantom block daylight along the shattered back wall. Ben had also seen it. He softly said, 'Belly down on the floor.'

They dropped down. Killian had fallen with one arm outstretched to support his head. He was watching the back wall.

He did not see the phantom, only his brief shadow as he leaned to see inside.

The ensuing few minutes were the longest Killian would ever remember.

The daylight-blocking wraith departed northward along the rear wall. He did not make a sound until he was at the far corner then he called something in a language none of the men lying on the cabin floor understood, but understanding was not necessary, the call was followed by men coming down the rearward slope.

Jawn would have arisen but Ben growled for him not

to move. This time when shadows blocked out daylight along the rear wall voices were not only loud, but two of them spoke in English.

One man said, 'Crazy damned fools.'

The other voice, deeper and quieter said, 'It wouldn't matter, they was done for either way. Go around front kick in the door . . . looks to me like someone's got a ground cloth flung over him.'

Killian did not blink until the shadows moved away from the shattered wall beside the boulder to allow light to return, he then rolled and came upright in one smooth movement. He stepped to the far side of the door and raised his six-gun.

Ben also arose, as did Jawn, but they positioned themselves along the south wall.

The wait seemed too long. No one tried the door. Someone outside mumbled indistinguishable words. A voice speaking English said, 'Where?'

The answer also came in English. 'North up the slope an' southward. Listen. Shut up an' listen.'

The trapped men also listened but could hear nothing. The renegades out front were silent so long Killian thought they might have gone away. They clearly hadn't. A man said, 'I don't hear nothin'. Break open the damned door.'

The first speaker replied sharply. 'You're half deef anyway. Look at them In'ians. They heard it too.'

The silence stretched out until two Indians spoke. One of them knew enough English to tell the pair of white renegades there were horses atop the slope passing through the timber.

The scornful man said, 'Loose horses. Ain't no one ever come up here except us. Kick open that damned door. I want to see who'n hell they was.'

An Indian moved away from the cabin scanning the rim. He stood back there for almost a full minute then spoke to his tribesmen. They moved away to also listen. One of the white men swore and kicked the door hard. It did not yield because of the *tranca* but its splintered wood slivered. The man kicked again, harder this time and more of the splintered wood broke loose. He called to his companion. 'You got long arms, Wallis. Reach inside and raise the draw bar.'

Evidently the man named Wallis did not move. He was with the Indians watching the timberline along the rim. His fellow renegade lost his temper. 'Gawd-dammit, Wallis, open the door! I know for a fact Hendry had a cache in there somewhere.'

One Indian made a trilling sound. He and the other Indians went to the northern end of the cabin, spoke briefly then started northward, occasionally looking over their shoulders.

The man named Wallis yelled at them. They ignored him and continued in the direction of their waiting horses. One buck halted looking rearward and upward. He said something to his companions, raised his Winchester and fired. Both the renegades near the door had to step out into the open to see what the bronco had fired at.

The fusillade of gunfire from the rim dropped the

Indian in his tracks. One shot dropped the renegade with the coarse voice who hadn't believed the Indians had heard anything. His friend, the man named Wallis, jumped close to the cabin, flattened there until an Indian yelled at him in English to run.

The Indian who had paused long enough to shout the warning was shot as he was turning to join his companions. The other Indians raced for the timber, none was hit.

Wallis remained flattened against the cabin. He saw the Indians disappear among the trees. It was too late to make the same run.

Inside, Ben, Jawn and Killian had listened only half ready to believe help had arrived in the eleventh hour. Jawn went to the front window and would have leaned out if Ben hadn't caught him by the shoulder to yank him away.

Whoever had been atop the rim stopped firing. The men in the cabin heard riders racing among the trees on the rim in the direction the Indians had fled. Ben went to the table, sat down and drank from a canteen, considered the four dynamite sticks and shook his head. Jawn said, 'Who in hell could that be?'

Ben answered sarcastically. 'Mister Killian's Santa Claus. How'n hell would I know?'

Jawn was not irritated. He said, 'I never knew his helpers rode horses an' used guns.'

George Killian went to the south side of the ruined door to look northward. What he saw was not fleeing Indians, it was someone up against the front wall like he was nailed there. Killian caught Ben's attention and gestured. Both the lanky man and the 'breed came over to lean hard until they could see the man outside. Ben straightened up and called out.

'You son of a bitch drop that gun. *You up against the wall out there. Drop it!*'

Wallis stiffened and turned his head. There was not supposed to be anyone alive in there. When he let the pistol fall it clattered against the log wall.

Ben raised the *tranca,* stepped outside and was raising his six-gun when Killian came through the door in a hurtling lunge that knocked the Arkansan down. In the scramble to catch himself Ben lost his pistol. Killian kicked it so hard it skittered ten feet.

Jawn stood in the doorway with his mouth hanging open. Ben got slowly to his feet. Wallis hadn't moved. The moment he saw Ben step outside he had trouble breathing.

Killian faced the lanky man, waiting, but Ben brushed himself off, reset his hat and went to retrieve his six-gun. He did all this without looking at any of them. But when he had holstered his weapon he crossed to the renegade, grabbed him by the shirt, dragged him to the open door and flung him inside.

Jawn remained back by the door, expressionless and silent. Killian did not re-enter until he had moved about thirty feet from the cabin to look up the slope. What he saw was three or four riders sitting like statues looking down toward the cabin. He recognized only one of them—Catlin.

He returned to the cabin, kicked a chair around and straddled it. He ignored Ben and Jawn and stared at the renegade. He had a question for the man. 'Who killed the old man and burned my cabins?'

Wallis was white to the hairline. 'The old man got hit in the leg an' went down . . . Hendry went over, stood over him an' shot him in the head. We all fired them cabins.'

Ben leaned against the boulder eyeing the renegade. 'Who shot that homesteader's woman?'

Wallis answered without hesitation. 'Hendry; she was slow makin' up a bundle of food.'

A slight shadow darkened the riddled door which was hanging ajar. Jawn said, 'You! Who are them others?'

Catlin ignored him. She hadn't understood a word he had said. She went over to Killian and spoke rapidly. Wallis watched and when she had finished he said, 'You understand her?'

Killian shook his head. 'Do you?'

'She said she went back for a wounded horse, took it down to Bridgerville, left it with the liveryman to be looked after, rounded up some townsmen she said had rode to your place after the raid, an' led 'em up here by trackin' you fellers.'

Ben switched his attention to the old woman. So did Jawn but neither of them said anything. Killian did though. First he asked the renegade what his name was, when the man answered Killian told him to tell the old woman the three of them would owe her for as long as they lived.

After the renegade had interpreted the old woman made a leathery grin and touched Killian's shoulder lightly with one hand. She then went back outside.

Ben straightened a chair around, sat down and stared at the renegade without speaking. Wallis looked at the one remaining chair. Killian spoke sharply. 'Stay on your feet. Hendry did all the killing, did he?' Killian pointed. 'That's Hendry under the ground cloth. Tell us again you didn't kill the woman.'

Wallis's eyes flickered from one of them to the other. 'Hendry told you different?'

He got no answer, just three stares.

'He told me to shoot her. He said she wasn't movin' fast enough.'

They continued to sit in silence for a long time, until Catlin appeared in the doorway to say something. Wallis interpreted. 'They're comin' back—most of 'em. Who the hell are they?'

Still no one spoke to him. No one spoke at all. Ben sat watching Killian, until George stood up and asked Jawn to fetch a lass rope someone had left on the south wall hanging from a wooden peg, then Ben arose looking pleased.

They took Wallis out front where riders were coming down off the slope and from the north. The men from the north were riding tired horses. They had closed faces.

Catlin leaned against the front of the cabin chewing something. Her beady black eyes missed nothing. She said something but this time the renegade did not interpret, he was watching the riders from the north, who pulled to a stop about fifteen feet from the men on foot and sat there in strong silence gazing at the renegade. One man who knew Ben fished a plug from a pocket and offered it. Ben went over, took the plug, looked at it and dryly said, 'Asa, carry 'em in your shirt pocket. This has got lint on it.' Ben then gnawed off a cud and cheeked it, handed back the plug and returned to the side of George Killian. Jawn stood behind them with the coiled lass rope.

The heavy man in front who had a gold chain across his ample middle dismounted and spoke quietly to George Killian. 'I knew that dead one. He came to the store a few times. I recognized him from the rim . . . Asa shot him. I don't believe I've seen this other one before.' Mister Bullock did not await any comment, he also said, 'We caught one and hung him back in the trees. One was shot through. Big In'ian. We left him to die. I think there was another one but we couldn't find no sign of him. You need anyone to help lean on the rope?'

Killian shook his head. As he, Ben and Jawn punched and pushed Wallis toward the northerly stand of trees the renegade looked over his shoulder and said something in a language only one person who heard him understood and Catlin continued to lean on the wall chewing. She did not call back. There was no reason for her to. Wallis had told her to tell her people how their friend had died. All Catlin did to indicate that she had heard was expectorate and watch the 'friend' of her people being led away to be hanged—among her people the worst of all ways for a man to die.

George had never participated in a lynching, had doggedly opposed even the idea of a hanging without a trial, but this time, with shadows lengthening he waited for Ben to select a tree with a stout lower limb, watched Jawn use the renegade's belt to secure his arms behind his back, and had the feeling these two had done this before—which they had.

Ben tossed the lass rope over the limb, tested both using his weight and when he was satisfied he nodded to Killian without looking at the renegade.

Wallis asked for something to drink. They had no liquor. He said he'd like to clear his conscience and while Ben looked grimly reluctant Killian nodded his head. Wallis would have rambled but Ben cut him short. He told the outlaw all he should ask forgiveness for right now was the killing of that homesteader woman.

Wallis eyed the Arkansan. 'You never killed nobody?' he said.

Ben's reply was cryptic. 'No one that didn't need it— an' none of 'em was women, you murderin' son of a bitch. Quit talkin' an' pray, that's what they usually do. As far as I know prayers never stopped a hanging. Get on with it!'

Wallis looked at the limb, at the noose dangling from it and closed his eyes. His lips didn't move, his expression didn't change. If he prayed, Ben, Jawn and Killian never knew.

When Ben's impatience got the better of him he caught hold of an arm, jerked the renegade under the limb and snugged up the lass rope noose. Wallis looked at each one of them, saving Ben for the last.

Jawn took the slack out of the rope, waited until Ben gestured for Killian to get a grip on the rope, then nodded as Jawn tightened the rope before taking position behind Killian.

Wallis was a stocky man. It required the combined strength of all three of them to hoist him off the ground, not very far but far enough. Wallis's entire body strained, his legs kicked wildly, he was choking to death, something which happened slowly, meanwhile the men on the tag-end of the rope had to brace themselves. Eventually the struggling eased but the legs spasmodically jerked, the body twisted first one way then the other way.

Ben gruffly said, 'Keep it tight an' walk toward the tree.' By the time they had made the rope fast around the tree the hanging man only strained and kicked feebly.

Killian turned his back. Jawn watched until the renegade went limp and barely turned. He looked at Ben, who said, 'Leave the son of bitch up there,' and started back toward the cabin.

The others were waiting. They had examined the inside of the cabin, had found Hendry Pickett, marveled at the bullet-riddled interior, saw the sticks of blasting powder on the table with the bloodstained scrap of paper, and returned to the fading day.

Catlin went inside too, after the others had left. She stood looking around, touched nothing and went out front at the sound of men talking.

Ben was brusque. He said the renegade was dead and as far as he was concerned he could hang in the tree until the wolves found him. Not many of the townsmen looked at Ben. They favored lynching when it was needed but beyond that they were not as unrelenting as the Arkansan. In fact, when the animals were rounded up and brought in, while the townsmen worked near Ben at rigging out, none of them spoke to him. If he noticed, and he probably did, it did not bother him at all.

Catlin edged close to Killian as they started away from the cabin. She smiled without speaking, which was just as well.

Dusk was on the way. From the rim Killian looked back; except for the boulder-smashed rear wall the clearing and its dilapidated cabins looked about as they had when he'd first seen them, and with failing daylight to enhance their appearance of serenity the clearing looked as it had over the years of abandonment.

Mister Bullock reined in beside Killian. He looked tired, rumpled and had a shadow of beard showing. He said, 'We buried Ambrose out behind where his cabin was.'

Killian nodded.

The storekeeper also said, 'I knew him from the store but not real well.'

131

Again Killian nodded. No one had known Ambrose real well, not even George Killian.

It became dark in the forest, their passage was almost noiseless. Eventually one of the townsmen, the man called Asa, reined back to tell the storekeeper there was a clearing ahead. He thought they should bed down there until daylight returned.

Ben heard and scowled. 'Ain't no need. If we keep goin' we can get down to Bridgerville before daybreak.'

No one dissented. The townsmen were hunched inside their jackets, riding like disembodied spirits. Action was invariably followed by reaction, they had seen enough of violence to last them a long time. They did not say much among themselves and completely ignored Ben and the storekeeper, even when the Arkansan beckoned Catlin forward and pointed to the ground. She understood his meaning and without even a grunt rode ahead to lead the way. It was too dark to read tracks but she never deviated from the route the town-riders had taken to reach the clearing. She had read sign to get them up there and some way or another followed the identical trail getting them down out of the highlands to open country where a healthy moon helped visibility the full distance to Bridgerville, which they reached with the night well advanced, cold and as still as death.

There were only one or two lights in the village. If anyone heeded the barking dogs their noise was of insufficient interest to arouse folks because no additional lights appeared.

Singly and in pairs the men turned off heading for their homes. The dogs continued to bark but that too lessened as time passed.

Killian stood beside the horse he had ridden gazing northward while Ben and Jawn off-saddled and led their animals to a pole corral to be fed.

It might have been imagination but Killian could have sworn he heard the distant, faint wail of a coyote.

11

The Last Ride

Asa, the townsman, met Killian outside the café and took him to breakfast, paid the bill and left Killian to go among the shacks at the lower end of town to find the Arkansan.

The Arkansan listened impassively to what Asa had to say, inclined his head once and went out back where Jawn was shaving, sat on a bench and said, 'Jawn, you need a woman.'

The 'breed's razor stopped in mid-air. He stared at the man on the bench.

Ben scuffed dirt and studied the designs he had made when he spoke again. 'Well, she saved our bacon; a man don't forget somethin' like that.'

Jawn, with a half-lathered face put the razor in its basin of warm water and said, 'That old In'ian?'

133

'She's the reason you'n me an' Mister Killian is alive.'

'She belongs to him. I don't.'

Ben arose, shoved Jawn out of the way and with an ancient grey towel around his shoulders went to work to lather his face as he said, 'We owe her, Jawn. What she done deserves whatever we can do for her.'

'She belongs to Mister Killian. What'n hell would we do with an old In'ian woman no one can understand?' Jawn brightened. 'She's got two horses. She can find her people an' with two horses some buck'd want her.'

Ben shaved in total silence. It was a painful procedure. Jawn went inside their shack to rummage for the only change of clothing he had. They were clean; he had scrubbed them in the creek east of town. As he was dressing a horse whinnied then kicked a slab of wood.

Jawn went out front to look northward. The liveryman, a sour, cranky man with sore feet had a horse cross-tied and was striking it with the handle of a hay fork. The animal fought back as well as it could but being cross-tied it couldn't do much but squeal and lash out.

Jawn watched while cinching his belt. He did not see the blur of movement until Killian caught the liveryman from behind, spun him around, wrenched the hay-fork from him and swung it.

Jawn's mouth dropped open. The liveryman bent double with one hand trying to shield his soft parts from another blow while his other hand rummaged in his clothing. Jawn knew what was going to happen and did not hear Ben come up behind him.

The liveryman had his belly-gun rising when Killian struck his arm with the hay-fork handle. Ben started up there as Killian dropped the hay fork, shoved the liveryman to a bench and pushed him down, turned his back to go and untie one of the ropes on the terrified, sweating horse. Behind him Ben said, 'What's the matter with you, Alec? That's a gentle mare.'

The liveryman was holding his middle with both hands when he looked up. 'I hate mares,' he said, breathing painfully.

Ben stood considering the man with sore feet. 'I've rode that mare. She's gentle as a dog. Now you're goin' to say she kicked you.'

'She did.'

Ben shook his head and turned where Killian was examining the animal. Anythin' serious, Mister Killian?'

George had a hand resting on the mare's back. 'She won't be fit to ride for a while. He was beating her over the back.'

Ben relaxed as Jawn came up, still not having cinched his britches. Ben said, 'Jawn, you want a horse?'

'I got a horse, Ben.'

'No. We got to take them animals back to that lady that loaned 'em to us.'

Jawn considered the mare. She was young enough to still have a round chin. She wasn't tall, maybe twelve hands. She was still sweating but no longer quaking. Jawn said, 'She belongs to Alec.'

Ben fished forth a darkly stained roll of greenbacks, untied the bills and with the liveryman's eyes rounded with surprise at the Arkansan having that kind of money, straightened on the bench as Ben said, 'How much for her, Alec?'

The liveryman's color was returning. 'She's a sound animal, Ben. Gentle as a lamb, a good ridin' mare an—'

'How much, you old son of a bitch?'

'Ben, I give twelve dollars for her from an In'ian. You can have her for—'

'You never paid twelve dollars for a horse in your life,' Ben exclaimed, but peeled off twelve dollars, tossed them in the dirt at the liveryman's feet and told Jawn to go take his mare out back of town where there was feed. Jawn obeyed. He'd once had a horse but it either ran away one night or was stolen. Twelve dollars was more money than Jawn'd seen in a long time.

Killian was not surprised at the roll of greenbacks but he was surprised at Ben's feeling about the beaten animal. Ben saw Killian staring and said, 'Somethin' about folks—them as don't have much use for human beings like animals. I expect you know by now how I feel about the two-legged critters.'

Alec picked up the twelve dollars and started back down his runway when Killian addressed the Arkansan. 'You like horses, Ben?'

The Arkansan's answer was brusque. 'Better'n most people, Mister Killian.'

'Then buy the livery barn. You and Jawn need something to work at.'

Ben considered George for a long moment before turning to the duck-walking man called Alec. 'Come back here, you old screwt.'

Alec turned apprehensively. 'Me?'

'Yes you.'

Alec duck-walked back outside and sank down on the bench. Ben and Killian eyed him stonily. Alec squirmed. 'Well, she was fixin' to kick me.'

Ben was unrelenting. 'Lyin' old bastard . . . Alec?'

'What?'

'You got no right to be around animals. How much for your barn'n the livestock that goes with it?'

The liveryman's mouth hung open and his eyes widened. He had known the Arkansan for years. During that time Ben had done odd jobs around Bridgerville and the countryside. He had never, to Alec's knowledge, had a second cent to bless himself with.

He licked his lips, shot a look at Killian over with the mare and back before he said, 'Ben, if I was to sell out I'd go down to Californey to see my daughter, and that's a hell of a distance to have to come back for my money . . . you can't afford—'

Ben leaned, dragged the liveryman to his feet and while their faces were close he said, 'How much!'

Alec shot Killian a frightened look and got back a totally uninterested and impassive stare. 'I ain't considered sellin' Ben. I'd have to figure on it.'

Ben let the liveryman slump back to the bench, turned and jerked his head. As he and Killian were walking away Ben looked back just once. 'Fifteen minutes, Alec.'

They were over in front of the general store when Catlin materialized as she often did, without a sound. Ben frowned. It had been his intention to go up to the saloon for an eye-opener. The saloonman did not allow women in his place of business, and certainly not Indians. The old woman was softly smiling at Killian. Ben said, 'What'er you goin' to do with her?'

Killian answered without hesitation. 'Feed her breakfast.'

Ben's eyes widened. 'Where?'

'The café.'

Ben's stare was fixed. 'She can't eat in there. She won't get past the door.'

Killian considered the lanky Arkansan. 'Do folks in this town have respect for you, Ben?'

'I expect so.'

'You go into the café with us, then.'

The lanky man reddened. His lips were compressed and he was about to speak when Mister Bullock came out of his store, saw them and approached smiling. He nodded to Catlin.

Ben said, 'He wants to take that In'ian to the café to be fed, Mister Bullock. The whole town'll faunch at the bit if he tries it.'

Mister Bullock, freshly shaven, wearing clean clothes

and the massive gold chain across his paunch, looked at the wizened little Indian woman and back to the Arkansan. 'Ben, I own the café building. Did you know that?'

Ben hadn't. 'No.'

Mister Bullock stopped smiling. He looked coldly at the Arkansan. 'But for that old woman you'n Jawn an' Mister Killian would be dead . . . do you know that?'

'Yes, dammit, I know it, but she can't go—'

'Yes she can,' the storekeeper said. 'Let's go see. Folks know by now it was her led us up there an' it was her saved the three of you from gettin' your heads split open. Let's go see, Ben.'

The Arkansan was reluctant enough to be the last to use the café entrance. Catlin was the first, propelled into that position by the storekeeper.

There were three rangemen at the counter, and the town blacksmith. The rangemen were eating; Asa was having only coffee.

The four of them turned, the caféman appeared from his cooking area, stopped dead still with a slow-gathering frown forming. He looked from Catlin to Mister Bullock, who pushed Catlin to the counter and sat her down as he said, 'I don't think she's had a decent meal in days, Ed. Make up a platter for her.'

The rangemen were watching the red-faced caféman. So was everyone else. He made one sputtering effort to protest and Ben interrupted him. 'Do it, Ed. No talk—just do it.'

Still the caféman did not move. He wiped both hands

139

on his apron until one of the rangemen, whose drawl was similar to the same way Ben spoke, but the difference was between an Arkansan and a Texan, said, 'You heard what she done, Ed? Well now, where I come from somethin' like that really matters. If you don't want to feed her, I'm a fair cook.'

As the Texan arose the caféman shot another look at Mister Bullock, wheeled and returned to his cooking area. He hadn't done what was customary, he hadn't put a cup of coffee before Catlin where she sat at the counter.

Mister Bullock went behind the counter, poured coffee into several cups, placed the first one in front of Catlin then shoved the others at Ben and Killian, keeping one cup for himself.

Catlin tested the coffee, made a face and pushed the cup away. One of the rangemen chuckled as he said, 'Sioux, ain't she? I spent a long winter one time trappin' up north with the Sioux.'

He leaned around his companions and said something that brought the old woman's head up and around, black eyes brightening. She said something back and the rangeman launched into a long harangue which only Catlin understood. He told her what her companions had done. She made a short statement and jutted her jaw in Killian's direction.

The rangeman turned and considered Killian, who was clearly not a stockman and who, in the eyes of the rangeman looked like a homesteader, toward whom rangemen were not friendly.

140

The cowboy said, 'Mister, she told me she lost her son.'

Killian nodded without speaking.

'She said you was now her son.' At Killian's uncomfortable look the cowboy said, 'Their customs ain't like ours. The spirit of her son is in you—some way—don't ask me how. Like I said, they ain't like us.'

The caféman returned with a platter of meat and potatoes. Under Mister Bullock's steady gaze he also got her a large slice of blueberry pie from beneath a fly-proof large glass bowl on the shelf behind the counter.

Ben gruffly said he'd be back directly and departed. Killian and the storekeeper sat at the counter on each side of Catlin who ate with both hands and a knife. Mister Bullock looked at Killian. 'Her son?'

George nodded for a refill and the caféman, flat-lipped and unhappy tipped the cup full again. The rangemen and Asa left about the time two burly, bearded freighters in heavy woollen shirts entered. One of them nodded around, saw Catlin and froze. He mumbled something to his friend before they both left the café.

The caféman had a throbbing vein in the side of his neck. He leaned across from the storekeeper and said, 'This is goin' to ruin my business.'

Mister Bullock didn't think so. 'You got the only eatery, Ed, an' folks get hungry. Besides, folks know what she did. I don't think it'll run off your trade. In fact, when folks come around you can tell 'em you felt honor-bound to feed her for what she did.' Bullock made a cold, small smile. 'You'll be a hero, Ed.'

The caféman clearly did not think so. He returned to his cooking area. The racket he made slamming pots and pans back there was an indication of how he felt.

Catlin heeded none of the noise. She cleaned the platter down to its worn, shiny base, reached for a water bottle and half drained it.

Killian was awed that so small and shriveled an individual could put away so much food.

Mister Bullock's clerk, a scarecrow of a man who wore black sleeve garters from wrist to elbow, came to tell his employer he was needed at the store.

After the storekeeper departed the caféman reappeared, clearly angry and hostile. He looked around, satisfied himself Killian and the old Indian were the only ones at his counter, removed his apron, yanked the empty plates from in front of Catlin and stormed to his cooking area where he put them aside and returned to raise his arm in the direction of the door as he said, 'Out! Damned squatter an' a squaw at the same time. *Out!*'

George sat gazing at the angry man, who was thick and burly—and punky soft. When the caféman came opposite Catlin and yelled at her to leave, she seemed to shrink. Killian stood up, leaned across the counter, got a handful of his shirt and pulled hard enough for the caféman to almost lose his footing. He squawked and raised a hand to free himself.

Catlin came off the bench with her knife rising. The caféman squawked louder, Killian released him and he fell against his pie table.

He glared at them both. The old woman held her knife gripped and ready. The caféman roared at them, 'I'll get the constable!' and straightened up to go back through his cooking area to the alleyway beyond.

George took Catlin by the arm, left the café and nearly collided with a tall, angular, greying woman carrying a net shopping bag.

The woman's eyes sprang wide. She made a noise in her throat and fled across to the far duckboards where she yelled to a lean, older man and pointed over where the old Indian woman was still clutching her knife.

The man hesitated as the woman swept past, poked his head past the saddle and harness-works doorway, spoke and started across the road.

Killian pushed Catlin behind him. She clung to the knife. It wasn't necessary to understand the language; that lean man's expression was hostile and his stride was forceful.

Killian did not wait to be attacked, he caught the older man with one foot raised to the plankwalk with a straight-arm strike. The lean man went down on his back, rolled and came part way up reaching beneath his coat.

A hard, drawling voice spoke from south of the café where a warped wooden overhang shadowed him. He said, 'Don't do nothin' rash, Herb,' and cocked the six-gun as he walked up.

The older man arose bringing roadway dust with him. He rocked his jaw with one hand while glaring at Killian. He said, 'Ben, you never did run with good company . . . now it's a homesteader and an old squaw.'

The Arkansan holstered his sidearm, stepped to the edge of the plankwalk and addressed the other older man. 'Go home, Herb.'

The other man was not ready to do that. He pointed to Killian. 'That gawdamned furriner—I know who he is, lives up a canyon with another reprobate named Ambrose—.'

'Go home, Herb!'

'That old witch was fixin' to attack my wife. She was holdin' that knife ready to use it.'

Ben stepped off the plankwalk, stopped directly in front of the other man and said, 'Where you been, Herb? You ain't heard what she done . . . go ask Mister Bullock.' Ben took hold of the man's arm and gave him a rough push in the direction of the general store, stood watching until the lean man was down as far as the store where he halted to glare back. Ben gestured to him. 'Ask Mister Bullock. Go on now.'

When the furious townsman entered the store Ben stepped back on to the plankwalk shaking his head. He did not comment on what had taken place, instead he said, 'Jawn'n me own the livery barn . . . I set him to cleanin' stalls. He didn't cotton to the idea until I told him he was half-owner an' it was about time he learned how to work.'

Ben looked at Catlin and winked. The old woman still had her teeth bared. While gazing at her he spoke to George. 'She'll come in handy up yonder when you

144

rebuild your cabin. She can cook an' all. In time you'll learn Lakota an' maybe she'll learn English—but I ain't real sure of that. Old dogs don't learn new tricks, do they?'

Killian stared at the Arkansan. Across the road the harness-maker, still wearing his waist-high, wax-stiffened apron, stood in overhang shade looking in the direction of the café. He had an old hawgleg pistol shoved into his waistband. It had been his intention to go to the assistance of the man whose wife had been frightened out of her wits by Catlin, but clearly the squabble was over. He turned to go back into his shop sighing with relief. He knew Ben Percival as well as anyone and better than most. He had no desire at all to be on Ben's wrong side in a scuffle.

They went down to the livery barn where Jawn was still maneuvering an old wheelbarrow from one stall to the next as he dunged out. He stopped when they entered the runway, grinned through sweat and abandoned his chore to walk back to a bench outside the harness room and ask Killian if Ben had told him they owned the livery barn. Before Killian could reply, Jawn made a wide sweep of the back of his neck with a faded old blue bandanna and addressed Ben wearing a frown.

'I thought you said we'd buy the saloon.'

Ben's reply was marginally sheepish. 'I did say that, but Alec beatin' that little mare changed my mind. But I'll tell you what we can do—we can save for a spell, put savings with what we got off them renegades an' still buy the saloon. You can run it.'

'What'll you do?'

'Stay with the livery barn. I'm fond of horses. You know that.'

Jawn sat gazing at the sweat-damp bandanna in his lap for a moment before speaking again. 'I don't want the saloon. We been partners a long time, Ben . . . I'll stay with you down here.'

When Killian looked around Catlin was gone. Jawn jerked a thumb toward the rear alley. 'She went out there. She's got a hurt horse in a corral back there.'

Killian found the old woman in the corral examining the wound on the horse they had found in the rocks with the dying Indian. He leaned on the stringers watching. She crooned to the horse, brought something greasy from among her clothing, patted it gently on the wound, and leaned against the horse, who was content to have a friend. She saw Killian and spoke, checked herself and used hand-language, which might as well have been Lakota. He smiled and shook his head. She smiled, turned back and pointed to the horse she had ridden from Bridgerville when she had led the town-riders up yonder. She said something about that horse too.

Both animals were logy from eating. There was clean water in a circular stone trough that leaked—not accidentally but on purpose; for a horse to drink it had to stand in mud which was the best thing for dry hooves. There was one drawback—mud daubers and wasps hovered in large numbers, and while they rarely stung animals, they would sting men.

Ben came out to also lean and look in at the old woman. He said, 'I give her that other horse.'

'Did you own it?'

'Yes. Alec said it went with the business.' Ben turned to face Killian. 'There's talk . . . Asa an' some of the others want to help you rebuild up yonder.' Ben paused to fish forth one of his rolls of greenbacks. He kept his head down as he peeled off greenbacks and said, 'This ain't a gift. It's what I figure you got comin' from what me'n Jawn got off them renegades. It ought to see you through next winter when your house is finished.'

Killian looked at the notes, some had dark stains on them. When he hesitated Ben punched them into Killian's pocket, turned and went back inside.

Catlin eventually crawled out of the corral and leaned beside Killian. She was chewing something, which did not matter, they could not converse anyway. But she placed a dark, worn old claw of a hand on his sleeve. Catlin was happy, something which hadn't happened often during her long life.

Killian stood motionless watching the torpid horses. What Ben had said might be true, she could cook and do chores for him—except for one thing he had thought about since standing above dead Ambrose, and at other times since, he did not know how to tell the old woman that he did not intend to rebuild in Killian's Canyon.

Jawn came to tell Killian a settler had ridden into town yelling that six renegades, four whites and two Indians had burned his barn, shot his little daughter, that he, his wife and their baby son, had hidden in a stone

147

cellar under the house until the renegades left taking the settler's team after they had looted the house.

Killian started for the barn with Jawn and Catlin following. He barely made it to the runway when Ben rode out the front entrance while several men and Mister Bullock were saddling when Killian reached them. They yelled at him to get mounted. Jawn was already hauling a saddle, bridle and blanket from the harness room.

As Killian went after a horse Catlin followed. She stopped him at a corral gate and handed him something. She was not smiling nor chewing. She didn't have to understand the language; she had seen many warriors in a hurry to get a-horseback with their weapons.

He shoved the trinket she had given him into a pocket, eased her aside and hurriedly brought a horse up to be rigged out.

12

Killian's Decision

Ordinarily when renegades struck they burned buildings, which made it easy for posse-riders. They could set a course by smoke. But these raiders had not started fires so it was up to the settler to take them by the most direct route, which he did, alternately leaning far over his horse peering ahead, or setting back in the saddle wringing his hands.

What particularly impressed George Killian was that the raid had occurred less than five miles from Bridgerville in open country in broad daylight.

When they reached the homestead the woman and a small boy were waiting. The little girl had been wrapped in a blanket. Her mother told the men from Bridgerville the little girl had been playing behind the barn, had only understood the homestead was being attacked when noisy men on horseback raced into the yard. She had run for the house. One of the renegades had shot her less than fifteen feet from the doorway.

Ben did not dismount, he listened, looked, jerked his head and left the yard leaning to the left to study the tracks.

After an hour he sent Jawn ahead to track, ignored the other riders, stood in his stirrups studying the country.

When he sat down he raised a rigid arm. A thin grey spiral of smoke was rising in the distance. Ben called Jawn back, left off tracking, set his course in the direction of the first few signs of a burning and made excellent time by going directly in the direction of the thinly rising smoke.

Killian was behind the Arkansan when faint sounds of gunfire reached him, reached them all.

Ben hooked his horse hard, the animal sprang out into a full run. The others followed. Mister Bullock called something to Asa who drew the saddle gun from its boot and rode with the butt against his upper leg.

When they were closer they could see a burning outbuilding, but evidently this homesteader had not been caught off guard. There were plumes of gunsmoke showing at several windows. Killian understood why the renegades had only fired an outbuilding, the people in the house were forted-up and fighting for their lives.

Ben drew his six-gun. The renegades were on foot fighting from various areas of cover. Ben called something to Jawn, who swerved northerly, widened the distance between himself and the others with Killian watching. He had no idea what Ben had sent the 'breed to do, but by now he knew the Arkansan did not do anything unless he had a reason.

The renegades were fully occupied firing at the house. Their kind normally avoided getting tied down, and certainly never on foot, but these attackers were firing furiously, making a small war out of what usually was a hit-and-run attack.

Ben gestured for the others to follow and reined off in the direction he had sent Jawn. Killian reasoned Ben's strategy was to come around the buildings behind the attackers. He may have been right but a tall Indian who was reloading, saw the racing riders. The men from Bridgerville could hear his howl over the gun-thunder. He was standing erect at the corner of a log barn gesturing and yelling.

For some time afterward it was not known who had shot him. It had been Jawn whose job was to find the horses and turn them loose. He was closest to his target when the Indian started gesturing and yelling. He had shot the bronco from a stand where he could place his Winchester in the notch of a log. It whittled down the odds. Killian had no idea who was in the house and there was too much smoke to make a count if he'd been able to make one, but as he and Ben rode abreast from behind the log barn two renegades abruptly turned and fired. The people in the house stopped shooting.

The fight had become between the men from Bridgerville and the renegades, who, as desperate men who knew they had nothing to lose, fought like demons.

Mister Bullock went off his horse, landed hard and rolled. Killian had no time to look; a renegade fired and tore the side of his coat. He could not see the shooter.

Ben did as he had done before, with his reins in his left hand and six-gun in the other hand, he rode directly where he had seen a muzzle blast.

The renegade was firing from the vicinity of the burning barn. He fired twice in quick succession and this time Ben sagged in the saddle but kept on riding. When he came close enough to feel heat he swung off his horse and with a bloody leg ran around behind the barn.

The renegade knew he would be flanked so he hastened to the northwest corner of the barn to greet the Arkansan when he appeared. He had made a fatal mistake, Jawn had a clear sighting, placed his Winchester in the notched log, took long aim and squeezed off a shot. The renegade had been crouching. When the bullet hit the man he was knocked forward. He fell in clear sight of Ben, who shot him twice before limping back where his horse should have been and wasn't.

Even a tethered horse will fight hard to get clear of fire. Ben hadn't tied the animal.

Killian was winged again by the renegade who, from hiding, had singled him out. This second strike drew blood across his shoulder. There was no immediate sensation of pain, that would come later.

Someone yelled from the house. Not only were the words indistinguishable but they were ignored.

George found cover where an unkempt old cottonwood tree stood. His personal adversary hit the tree then did not fire again. George was on the far side of the tree.

There was an inexplicable lull, partly because men were reloading, partly because the renegades could no longer find targets.

Ben yelled. 'You got a choice. Throw down your guns or get hung when we catch you.'

The reply was loud and defiant. 'You ain't goin' to catch nobody.'

That defiant shout came only moments before Jawn said, 'Mister, I got your brother. I'll kill him if you keep fightin'.'

This prolonged the lull. Two renegades started filtering from shelter to shelter to reach the area Jawn had called from. Killian had a glimpse of one man as he crossed a short open space. He was thick and unshaven and wild-eyed. He moved too fast for Killian to get off a shot.

In the bitter silence Killian heard a door slam. He was exposed in the direction of the house so he edged far-

152

ther around the old tree and looked back. If someone had come out of the house there was no sign of him. A man, in fact two men, had indeed left the house but by a rear door, not the one Killian could see.

Mister Bullock had crawled to shelter somewhere which meant he probably hadn't been hit hard.

What caused the lull to continue was the distinct sound of running horses. Killian thought Jawn had accomplished his purpose—to find the renegades' animals and free them.

There was an abrupt, very fierce exchange of gunshots where Killian thought Jawn was sheltered. It was a furious but brief exchange.

Killian figured his chance of reaching the outbuilding where Jawn had been firing from, decided if he could sprint fast enough he could make it. What he hadn't included in his guesswork was that the lull had gone on long enough for everyone to be reloaded and ready.

He ran as hard as he could, was almost to the log outbuilding when the gunfire brisked up. One slug tore the heel off his boot, which made him stagger and stumble. The second shot was better, it shot his little finger off as neat as a whistle.

He flattened to use a bandanna to tie off the wound.

Someone shouted from the south side of the yard where a smoke-house stood. There were two shots then brief silence until the man who had shouted clearly said, 'Drop it. Now help your friend stand up.'

The lull returned. Killian's hand was a bloody mess. He did as much as a one-handed man could do to cinch

153

off the bleeding, which was not enough.

Jawn appeared sidling around the log wall poking a renegade ahead with a cocked six-gun. The renegade was not tall and he had a slit of a mouth and venomous pale eyes. He also had a bleeding wound where his hat should have been.

It was over. The two men from the besieged house, a rugged, stalwart man and a lithe much younger one who was the spitting image of the older man appeared behind one renegade, a white man, helping another renegade, an Indian who could barely walk. He had been shot in the body.

Jawn's captive watched and missed nothing when Jawn moved to look at Killian's hand. The man broke away in a furious run. Jawn turned, watched for a moment, settled his six-gun across one arm, tracked the renegade and shot. The man ran forward right down to the ground.

Jawn leathered his weapon, took a tie-down thong from the bottom of his holster, looped it, tightened it until the bleeding stopped, then tied it off hard and fast.

The homesteaders crossed the yard where Jawn and Killian were standing. The Indian a renegade was supporting abruptly buckled at the knees and crumpled. The homesteader and his son leaned, flopped the Indian over, turned their backs and continued toward Jawn and Killian. The Indian was dead.

Two women emerged from the house carrying rifles. The homesteaders turned on them angrily. 'Get back inside! What the hell do you think you're doing? Get back in there an' bar the door.'

The women retreated. In the ensuing stillness the sound of a *tranca* being dropped into place was clearly audible.

The homesteader looked at Killian's hand. He was about to speak when Asa and the storekeeper walked up. Asa was supporting Mister Bullock who had a broken arm up high, above the elbow. The bleeding had been tied off but the storekeeper was covered with blood and looked very tired.

Ben was the last to arrive. He had tied off his bloody upper leg with a bandanna and a green stick. He limped up holding the twig; it provided the leverage to halt the bleeding. Jawn went to the Arkansan and would have fretted over the bloody leg but Ben growled him away, looked at the survivors and asked if the homesteader had any whiskey. The man nodded and hurried in the direction of the house.

While he was gone Ben said, 'How many got away?'

No one knew if any had gotten away so Ben sent Jawn to make a count. While the 'breed was gone Ben leaned on the log building and said, 'He's a good shot. Mister Killian, what happened to your hand?'

'I had a finger shot off.'

'Which finger, Mister Killian?'

'The little finger on my left hand.'

'Looks like the bleedin's been stopped.'

'It has.'

'Little fingers ain't much force anyway, Mister Killian. It's good it wasn't your trigger finger.'

Jawn returned about the same time the homesteader arrived with a bottle of whiskey. Ben took the first drink and passed it around. The last man to drink was Asa. He upended the bottle, only drops came out.

Jawn and the homesteader's boy went after the horses. One was missing. The homesteader offered one of his horses. Asa accepted, said he'd fetch the horse back when he could, and as they all got astride—Ben growling when Jawn offered to help him—two women came from the house, one carrying a tray of tin cups, the other one, older, had a jug of lemonade.

They drank the pitcher empty. When the woman offered to make more Ben shook his head, brushed his hatbrim, forced a smile and jerked his head.

Killian looked back from several hundred yards out. The homesteaders were still standing there, looking southward. Jawn said, 'He ain't goin' to thank us tomorrow. It's hard work diggin' graves.'

They had Bridgerville in sight before Ben spoke. 'One of 'em got away.'

Asa nodded agreement. 'On one of your livery horses, Ben.'

The townsfolk were silent as they watched the riders pass down the main thoroughfare. Several women clanned together to make the firehall ready for the injured. One woman in particular, was busy caring for her father's swollen, gory-looking arm and the equally gory-looking left hand of George Killian. Once, when she was caring for her father Mister Bullock beckoned for her to lean and whispered.

She took a basin of pink water and a dry towel over to Killian and amid lamentations over his injury, asked if he would stay in town until the hand was healed.

He smiled slightly and shook his head. 'I'm obliged for all you've done, Myrtle, but I won't be staying.'

She cocked her head sympathetically. 'Papa told me about the old man—Ambrose—an' what they done to your cabins, but with summer passing an' you one-handed—'

She was interrupted and rudely shouldered aside as Catlin appeared. She looked at Killian's shirt, at his freshly bandaged hand with blood seeping through and said something. He looked blank so she rummaged his pockets found what she sought and held it up.

One of the older women, spare, weathered and square-jawed came over to say, 'She told you that little piece of rawhide with strong medicine inside kept you from getting killed. She said you must always carry it with you.' The woman paused to fix Killian with a hard stare. 'She said you belong to her. That her son's spirit lives in you. Mister Killian?'

'Yes'm.'

'Wherever you go she will go.'

George saw Catlin's bright gaze, her expression of fondness. He spoke to the hard-faced, older woman. 'I am going back where I came from; where I belong. I can't take her. She would be lost in Ireland. How do I tell her that?'

The hard-faced woman's reply was blunt. 'I don't know,' she said and walked away.

157

Myrtle Bullock stood like a stone looking from one of them to the other. She felt tears coming and turned to go back where her father was. There, she cried.

Mister Bullock soothed her with his uninjured arm and said, 'Things don't always come out right. He didn't want you?'

'It's the old In'ian. She thinks he's her son come back. . . . Papa, he's going to leave . . . go back to Ireland. It's going to break the old In'ian's heart. Papa, can we take her in? She has no one. She saved their lives up yonder. She . . . she's an old woman without kin, without no one after George leaves . . . Papa?'

Her father looked over where Catlin was fussing over Killian. 'We'll take her in,' he told his daughter.

George Killian left Bridgerville with Catlin's amulet in his pocket. He carried it for the rest of his life.

Catlin would go of an evening and sit on the ground looking eastward, the direction Killian had taken. She had nodded understanding when the hard-faced woman was brought to explain to her that George had gone far over the sea to his native land.

She sat dry-eyed and barely rocking back and forth every night until the chill arrived then she returned to the Bullock house.

She ate well, occasionally smiled but in most ways she had turned inward. She was with the Bullocks three weeks. One bright autumn morning she was gone. So were her two horses. Jawn had been at the barn when she had arrived, wordlessly led out her animals, mounted the sound one, led the one with the healing hip and had ridden northward up the back alley in the direction of the distant mountains.

Myrtle Bullock wanted to go after her. Myrtle's father shook his head. 'You won't find her. They cover tracks better'n a squirrel. But even if you found her, Myrtle, she won't come back . . . an' it's best. She's full-blooded In'ian; old one at that. They just plain don't never settle among us whites.'

'But Papa, she's old, something could happen—'

'Myrtle, I been around them some. I'd say she maybe wants something to happen to her. I'm sorry, honey. You can't go.'

Center Point Publishing
600 Brooks Road ● PO Box 1
Thorndike ME 04986-0001 USA

(207) 568-3717

US & Canada:
1 800 929-9108